PROJECT JACKALOPE

PROJECT JACKALOPE

Emily Ecton

chronicle books · san francisco

To my teachers: Queen Eleanor, BJ Davis,
Gloria Needlman, Lilla Fano

And all teachers who encourage kids to write.

Library of Congress Cataloging-in-Publication Data:
Ecton, Emily.
    Project jackalope / by Emily Ecton.
      p. cm.
    Summary: When Jeremy is entrusted with Professor Twitchett's creation, a jackalope,
he must find a way to keep it safe from the government agents who want it for their
own purposes.
    ISBN 978-1-4521-0155-2 (alk. paper)
    1. Science projects—Juvenile fiction. 2. Neighbors—Juvenile fiction. 3. Science
fairs—Juvenile fiction. 4. Friendship—Juvenile fiction. [1. Animals, Mythical—
Fiction. 2. Science projects—Juvenile fiction. 3. Neighbors—Juvenile fiction.
4. Science fairs—Juvenile fiction. 5. Friendship—Juvenile fiction.] I. Title.

PZ7.E21285Pr 2012
 [E]—dc23

2011025404

Book design by Aimee Gauthier.
Typeset in Atma Serif.

Manufactured in China.

10 9 8 7 6 5 4 3 2 1

Chronicle Books LLC
680 Second Street, San Francisco, California 94107

www.chroniclekids.com

jack·a·lope \ja-kə-lōp\

noun (plural jack·a·lope or jack·a·lopes)

Definition:

1) A mythical animal resembling a rabbit but with the antlers of an antelope, goat, or deer

2) Horned creature depicted in the folklore of the American West, most notably Wyoming [likely origin]

3) A crossbreed of a rabbit and antelope

4) An imaginary animal, e.g., unicorn, Sasquatch, and Loch Ness monster

See illus.

1.

Gross Candy Weakens My Defenses

First off, I should apologize to Safety Officer Webber. After eight straight years of Student Safety Days and Stranger Danger warning checklists, you'd think I'd be able to recognize a red flag when I saw one. But no, when confronted with an actual real-life threat, I totally missed it.

Just so you know—it's not like I'm a total loser. I'm not saying I'm brain surgeon material or anything, but I'm pretty much one of your basic junior high types. You know, there's the brainy kid, always getting extra credit and ruining the grading curve. Then there's your typical sports star, always breaking records and getting clapped on the back or patted on the butt in the hallway. And then there's that guy in the back of the class, inspecting a Life Saver covered in pocket fuzz and trying to decide whether it's too gross to eat. That kid? That would be me.

I only mention the Life Saver because that's what I happened to be focused on the day that I missed the warning signs. It seemed important at the time. The Life Saver in question was at least six months old and, as I ultimately decided when I got home, not too gross to eat. (I was wrong about that, too.)

So when I bumped into the strange man in the suit taking pictures of our mailboxes, he didn't really register. And believe me, he should've, because this building is on the National Registry of Boring, it's so lame. In this place, a guy in a suit is big news. But no, I didn't wake up to what was happening until I saw the second man. And I was trapped.

So, as I'm sure Safety Officer Webber would tell you, I had every reason in the world to be on high alert when I came inside and barreled into Mr. Suit. But instead, I bounced off of him like a volleyball, patted Boris the hallway gargoyle on the head, checked his mouth for a not-so-secret secret message (blue paper, which meant a message for me from my weird neighbor, Professor Twitchett), popped the filthy candy into my mouth, and then spent the trip up the stairs gagging and looking for a place to spit it out.

It wasn't until I'd decided to sacrifice Professor Twitchett's note and was in the act of spitting the slimy candy into the paper that I was even aware of the footsteps behind me. *Right* behind me. I heard them just a second before I felt the man's breath on the back of my neck.

The muscles in my back immediately tensed up, and it was all I could do not to break into a run. Because breath on the neck means you're close. Too close. Closer than any normal person gets. I crushed the note and stuffed it into my pocket and gave a casual glance behind me, kind of an unspoken "Hey, bub, back off" kind of glance. The man's mouth curved into a smile. I'm guessing I don't have to tell you it wasn't a friendly smile.

This would be a good time to tell you that I'm not easily freaked out. I watch horror movies with the best of them and only have two, maybe three nights of nightmares afterward. I can take it, that's what I'm saying. But when that man smiled at me, I had to suppress a full-body shudder.

I gave a tough-guy nod and strolled casually to my door. That's what I was going for, anyway. But I know that if I'd been auditioning for the role of me, I would never have been cast in the part. Putting my hand in my pocket, getting out my keys—everything I did felt completely stiff and unbelievable. I just knew I looked like a total phony.

It wasn't until I got to my door and glanced back down the hallway that I saw the second man. He was wearing a suit, too, just like the first one, and he was standing at the opposite end of the hall, watching me with cold, hard eyes. Not doing anything else, just watching.

I forced myself to look away and focus on the keys in my hand. I unlocked my door, taking my time and deliberately not looking at either Mr. Suit. But as soon as the door was open, the panic took over and I lurched inside. I slammed the door shut and double-bolted it, trying not to think about what I'd seen as I'd hurried inside. The first man, the one on the stairs, hadn't moved at all.

He was still just standing at the top of the stairs, watching me, with that smile on his face.

I eyed the dining room table. It looked too heavy for me to move in front of the door myself. The double lock would have to be enough. I put my ear up to the door, but I couldn't hear anything from the hallway. Well, nothing but that I've-got-my-ear-up-against-something ocean noise. I don't know what I was expecting anyway. I was just being paranoid. Too many scary movies, maybe. They probably weren't even there anymore. I was being such a wuss, getting all worked up over a couple of weirdos.

The thing was, it just didn't make sense for them to be here. Confession time—my building isn't really on the National Registry of Boring. It's not on anything. And there's nobody here that guys like that would want to visit. On the first floor, you have Mrs. Simmons, who doesn't have all her socks in the drawer, if you catch my drift. (If you don't, I mean that she's a little bit crazy.) As far as I can tell, she doesn't leave the building, ever. Not since the day she moved in. Maybe not in her whole life, if I had to guess. (Well, except for that moving-in part. Which actually wasn't that long ago, now that I think about it.)

Across the entryway from her, you have Agatha Hotchkins and her mom. Agatha's in my grade, and with her personality, it's not like she gets a ton of visitors. I'll just leave it at that. (Okay, let's put it this way. If Agatha had seen my crusty old Life Saver, she would've had to pull out a Life Saver at least two years older, covered with pocket lint, mold, and maybe even some snot for good measure.) Agatha's the one who had the bright idea of leaving color-coded secret notes for each other in the mouth of Boris the concrete gargoyle downstairs. Except secret notes aren't that much fun when they're sitting right out there where anyone can see them. And when you're not really friends with the person you're getting notes from. (And when you're over seven years old.)

So a fancy Suit guy visiting one of them? Not likely. And I don't know that I'd call what those Suit guys were doing visiting anyway.

Upstairs, it's just me and my parents, Professor Twitchett down the hall, that flight attendant lady who's never home, and the couple across the hall from us, the

Garcias, the ones that make cookies on Saturdays. Mr. Garcia is your basic khaki-wearing office worker type. He's also the in-bed-by-nine type, so not a huge collective social life happening on the second floor either. (Well, I can't really say about the flight attendant lady. But for the sake of argument, let's just assume she's a social outcast too.) So it's not like Mr. Suit would want to hang out with anybody upstairs. Unless the flight attendant lady has some kind of secret crazy wild life that I know nothing about, which I guess is possible.

It was probably all a big mistake. Wrong address or something. But I double-checked the door handle to make sure it was locked, just in case.

I shrugged off my jacket and went to get a drink to get the gross Life Saver taste out of my mouth. I was on my third swig from the orange juice carton when I remembered Twitchett's note.

I groaned. Whatever it said, I wasn't doing it. That was all there was to it.

A few months ago, Professor Twitchett adopted me as his personal errand boy. It used to be Agatha, but they had some kind of falling-out. I don't know what she did exactly, but it had to be pretty bad, because Twitchett completely banned her from his apartment and doesn't even speak to her now. He even changed the locks. (Which made me laugh, because really, Twitchett? Changing locks? Agatha's been able to pick locks since fourth grade, and Twitchett was the one who taught her. I know because that was her end-of-the-year show-and-tell project. Went over like gangbusters.)

I pulled the spitty note out of my pocket and shook the Life Saver remnant into the trash. Then I smoothed the wrinkles out and read it. Twitchett's always had his quirks, using code names and whatever, so I figured it would be typical Twitchett, weird and random and totally out there. But it wasn't what I expected.

Igor, (My code name. Don't ask.)
Please excuse my presumption, but I took the liberty of breaking into your apartment while you and your parents were out. You will understand that I had no choice but to leave one of my experiments in your care.

Guard it well.

TELL NO ONE.

I will be in touch to retrieve it soon.

Prof. FrankenTwitch

Make no mistake—No one includes our friend Agatha.

I crumpled up the note and threw it into the trash, trying not to notice how big the apartment suddenly felt. Twitchett had been in here. Without anyone knowing. He'd left something. And I had a bad feeling I knew where.

My bedroom door was open just a crack, which definitely wasn't the way I remembered leaving it. I crept up to the door and listened carefully.

Let me just be blunt—Twitchett is kind of a wack job. He's always talking down to me like I'm this stupid kid and acting like his errands are all important and top secret. You know, here's the cash, use this code name, don't be seen talking to me, come in through the back, blah blah secret spy blah. Like anybody cares if I go buy him a package of cotton balls and peroxide, right? He thinks that the made-up secret junk is the whole reason I do it, but really I'm in it for the extra cash he slips me when I come back with his top secret tube of Preparation H. (He said it was for the baboons at the zoo, but come on.)

So leaving secret notes and hiding things in weird places? Typical Twitchett. But he'd never actually broken into my house before. It creeped me out.

I listened until I felt like my ears were going to pop off, and then I carefully pushed the door open with the toe of my sneaker. At first glance the room looked just like I'd left it that morning—pile of clothes by the hamper, papers all over the desk and chair, comforter partway on the floor. It wasn't until I was kicking the comforter out of my way that I realized everything was all wrong. That comforter had definitely been all the way on the floor when I left. I remember, because I caught my shoe on the edge of it on my way out and dragged it behind me for a couple of steps. I froze and stared at the comforter like it was going to jump me, but it just lay there like, well, a comforter.

Taking a deep breath, I edged over to the bed and poked at the comforter with one finger. It was draped over what looked like a shoebox. Except bigger, so maybe for boots.

I clenched my fists. Twitchett had no right stashing his weirdo experiments in my bed. And why would he even do that? Just because his apartment was too much of a pigsty? (Yeah, I know, pot calling the kettle black. Don't start.) And knowing him, it was probably something foul-smelling or slimy that he'd read about online. I'd probably have to fumigate the room. Get a new mattress, at least. Well, that was it. Extra cash or no extra cash, I was done. He could get the Garcias to run his dumb errands from now on.

I was already planning my angry rant as I scooped up the box and opened it. And then closed it again. Quickly. Because whatever I expected, it wasn't this. I never expected Professor Twitchett's experiment to stare back at me. And blink.

2.

What Big Ears You Have

I think I should take this opportunity to apologize to Coach Reynolds, too. A couple of months ago, he made us learn these deep-breathing exercises, mostly because Huey Langford kept hyperventilating when it was his turn to climb the rope. (He's got this thing about ropes. You don't want to know.) Me and Clint Warburton practically busted a gut laughing at how lame the exercises were, and had to do some pretty fast talking to keep from getting sent to the office. But I have to hand it to the Coach: Those exercises sure came in handy when I opened that box. I went through the whole routine—deep, cleansing breaths; finding my center; even the head between the knees move, and when I felt ready, I cracked the box again. The thing inside blinked again.

I slammed the lid back down and went back into the head between the knees pose.

In the split second before that blink, I'd seen what looked like Twitchett's handwriting on a piece of paper in the bottom of the box. Which figured—leave it to Twitchett to write out an explanation and then hide it underneath some weirdo box creature. Don't get me wrong, I would've liked to know what it said. But with old Blinky guarding it, I was perfectly willing to stay in the dark.

Now just let me reemphasize here that it's not like I'm a total wuss or anything. The thing in that box wasn't your basic lab rat. I'm used to lab rats. I used to have one—a white one with pink eyes, named Killer. But the thing in the box wasn't anything like Killer. It wasn't like anything I'd ever seen before.

I was just about to go for round three with the thing in the box, maybe do a snatch and grab to get that note, when I heard the front door slam.

"Jeremy, I'm back!"

Right off I knew something was up. My mom was using her high fakey voice, and that's never a good sign.

"He should be right around here, Mr. . . . what did you say your name was?"

The hairs on the back of my neck prickled. Mom wasn't alone. And I had a feeling I knew who was with her.

I peeked out through the crack under the door. I couldn't see much, just a foot and part of a suit leg, but it was enough for me to put things together. I hadn't been involved in any criminal activity, I wasn't in trouble at school, and I hadn't even responded to that Nigerian banker guy who e-mailed me. I could only think of one reason some weirdo Suit guy would be coming to visit, and it had just blinked at me twice. All of Twitchett's top secret drugstore runs suddenly seemed a lot less innocent than they had before.

I cussed Professor Twitchett out in my head. The easy thing to do would be just to hand over the box and be done with it. Mr. Suit problem solved, Blinky-in-the-Box problem solved, everybody's happy.

"Jeremy?" Mom tapped on my door.

If that one Suit guy hadn't had such a smarmy attitude, maybe I would've. Maybe if he hadn't stared at me and given me that creepy smile. It definitely would've been the smart thing to do. But no one's ever accused me of being smart. I didn't know what Twitchett had saddled me with, but there was no way I was going to let those jerks from the hallway get their hands on it. At least not until I knew what I was dealing with. And if I handed it over right away, I might never know. I didn't want to end up that ancient guy with his teeth in a glass, muttering about the blinky thing he'd just handed away sixty years ago. I had to hide that box.

I scanned the room and my heart sank. Because trust me, there are no good hiding places in my room. (And let me tell you, I've looked.) But anyplace had to be better than my bed, right?

I rushed over to my clothes hamper, which thankfully was mostly empty, and put the box at the bottom. Then I scooped up my dirty gym suit, underpants, and socks from the floor and dumped them in on top of it.

I figured whatever was in that box had a good ten minutes before it suffocated under my dirty clothes, fifteen if it took shallow breaths until it passed out from the stench. It would have to be good enough.

I slammed the lid down on the hamper just as Mom pushed my door open.

"You okay in here?" she said with an awkward half smile. "We've got a visitor, hon. Could you come out for a sec?"

I nodded and let her push me out into the dining room by the shoulder. I tried to keep a poker face and act cool, but there was something about seeing Mr. Suit-from-the-Top-of-the-Stairs in my apartment that made me want to barf.

Mom nudged me encouragingly. "Jeremy, this is Mr. Jones."

I nodded and tried not to roll my eyes. Mr. Jones. Obviously a fake name.

"Mr. Jones here is a lawyer. Apparently Professor Twitchett has come into some money." Mom tried to nudge me closer. Not that it would do any good, though. My feet had turned into chunks of lead the minute I saw him. "Isn't that exciting, Jeremy?"

I shrugged. Lawyer my butt. He had to be a cop or something. Gangster maybe. Mafioso. Nothing good.

"That's right." Mr. Jones smiled at me. "I think Professor Twitchett will be very pleased. I just need to locate him and have him sign a few papers to transfer the funds. But he doesn't seem to be home. Do you know where he might be?"

He smiled again, and I'm sure it was supposed to suck me in. But it didn't. I shrugged again and didn't say anything.

Mom frowned at me and put her hand on my shoulder. I had a feeling I was going to get the rudeness lecture later on. She smiled up at Mr. Jones. "Well, I haven't seen him today, but he works at the zoo. He's a researcher? Something like that. Did you try his work?"

Mr. Jones didn't even look at Mom; he just kept staring at me. "He wasn't at the zoo. He seems to have just . . . disappeared. Poof!" He gave a short barky laugh that made both me and Mom jump a little. "I thought he might have communicated with your boy. He and the Professor are quite close, I understand?"

Why he would understand anything like that I don't know, since all I do is run Professor Twitchett's errands. Monkeys in Japan can do that—I know, I read about it in the paper. And it's not like me and Twitchett ever hung out. Not like he did with Agatha. Heck, I'm not even supposed to make eye contact with him in public.

Mom frowned. "I don't know that I'd say 'close' . . ."

I cleared my throat. "Sorry, I don't know where he is."

The man's eyes narrowed. "He hasn't communicated with you at all? That seems strange. Not even a . . . note, perhaps?"

I could feel sweat beading up at my hairline. Curse Agatha and her stupid totally-not-secret secret note system. He knew everything. He probably even knew about the thing in my room. And if I didn't watch it, I'd give myself away, and he'd pull out his cop handcuffs and throw me in jail for obstruction, or harboring a blinky thing or something. The situation was extreme. I took a deep breath and pulled a Dewey.

Dewey Childress is the biggest brain-dead jock in my English class. Most of the time, he looks like he's asleep, even when his eyes are wide open. Either that or he's a zombie. He's doing well to keep the drool in his mouth, that's what I'm saying. I don't know how he made it into junior high.

I did my best Dewey impression and gave a half smile. "Sorry, he didn't say anything." I tried to make my eyes glaze over, but I don't know if it worked.

"I find that extremely difficult to believe, son." It's not like Mr. Jones was being anything but polite, but I've never been more glad to have my mom in the room. I could see the muscle working in his jaw, and I knew he'd seen through my whole Dewey act. Mom must've noticed something was off, too, because she took a half step in front of me.

"Well, sorry we couldn't be of more help. If we see him, we'll be sure to tell him you came by. Maybe we could give him your card?"

Mr. Jones stared at me for a long second and then smiled at Mom. "I'm sure I'll see you again." He nodded at me silently and then let himself out. Without giving us a business card, I noticed.

The door had hardly shut before Mom smacked me on the shoulder. "How do you like that, huh? Inheritance. Must be nice. Don't you wish it was us he was looking for?" She grinned at me and headed into the kitchen.

I shrugged again. That was the last thing I'd want. "Yeah, I guess."

"You all ready for school tomorrow?" Mom said, grabbing a baby carrot from the fridge. "Homework done, tests studied for?"

"Not really." I started for my bedroom. "Big project, actually."

"Well, get cracking!" Mom said, crunching on the carrot. "First thing after dinner I want you hitting the books. Now help me set the table. Your dad will be here with the pizza any minute."

"Oh. Great," I said, taking the handful of silverware she handed me. Nothing like laying out forks while God knows what destroys your room. I don't think I've ever had a harder time choking down pizza. Seriously, I think I only managed four pieces.

As soon as everybody was done, I hustled into my room and closed the door. The hamper was still the way I'd left it, so I figured that was a good sign. What I needed to do was figure out what that thing was (if it had survived the underwear fumes) and get Twitchett to take it back. ASAP. Because if there was one thing I knew about creeps like Mr. Jones, it's that they don't give up. He'd be back.

I took a deep breath and took the lid off of the hamper, flinging it onto the bed so I couldn't wuss out again. Which was a big mistake. Because when I looked inside that hamper I almost lost it.

In my defense, I think anyone would have. I distinctly remembered putting my gym clothes on top of the box, right? I know I did that. But when I looked in the hamper, there were no gym clothes. There wasn't even any box—just a big pile of shredded cotton, pieces of cardboard, and that thing blinking up at me from the bottom of the hamper. I couldn't pretend it wasn't happening.

That thing, the one that had destroyed the contents of my hamper in what, thirty minutes flat? It was a bunny.

Yeah, I know. A tiny little fluffy bunny with soft tufty feet and huge Hallmark card eyes. Oh yeah, and a set of nasty-looking razor-sharp antlers coming out of its head.

It was a jackalope.

3.

I Hit the Bottle and Decide I Need Help

I may not be brain surgeon material, but the minute I saw those antlers, I knew that was no normal bunny. And yeah, I know what you're thinking. You're thinking, *Jeremy, get a grip. Jackalopes are imaginary. Everybody knows there aren't really bunnies with giant antlers. They're mythological. They don't exist, you wacko.* And that's what I was thinking, too. Except that's not so easy to remember when you have one sitting in your hamper with a piece of what used to be your underwear hanging off one antler.

So I did what any normal person would've done. I screamed and lunged for the cell phone. (Not a full-throated scream or anything. More like a manly stifled squeal.)

I'll tell you one thing. Mr. Jones may be the creepiest loser jerk of a gangster-cop-whatever, but he isn't a liar. Because he was right—Professor Twitchett was nowhere to be found. His home phone just rang and rang and his cell phone went right to voicemail every time. And it's not like I gave up after one call either. I can be pretty persistent when I've got a mythological creature on my hands.

"Professor Twitchett, it's Jerem—uh, Igor. Hi. I really can't keep this . . . uh . . . project here. Sorry. Call me back."

"Hi, Professor Twitchett, me again. I need you to call me right now. And there was a man here for you? Call me back. It's urgent."

"This isn't funny, Professor Twitchett! I can't sleep with this thing here, okay? Call me!"

I have to admit the calls were a little emotional by the end. It wasn't easy to stay calm and rational. But after about fifty calls, I decided I needed to man up and face the situation. Assess the facts. That kind of thing. Fact number one: Professor Twitchett probably wasn't going to answer the phone or call me back. Fact number two: I had a possible jackalope in my clothes hamper. Fact number three: Fact number two was practically guaranteed to get me grounded, arrested, or put into the psych ward.

I figured the sane and rational thing to do was to go online and make sure that what we had here was an actual jackalope situation. Because there was always a chance that it could be something else, like some kind of novelty robot toy, maybe. Maybe a jackalope-shaped Roomba vacuum cleaner? You never know. And here I'd be getting all worked up for nothing.

Well, guess what? They don't make jackalope-shaped Roomba vacuum cleaners. Or jackalope novelty robot toys. Jackalopes don't even show up in most of the online dictionaries. Apparently there are bunnies out there with some weird disease that makes people think they're jackalopes, but sorry, they didn't look anything like the picture-perfect model chowing down on my jockstrap.

There weren't a lot of options left. It was pretty much jackalope or nothing. I mean, Wikipedia doesn't lie, right? And believe me, I wish it did, because I wasn't all that thrilled with what I found out about our friend the jackalope.

Number one: They drink. I mean booze, the hard stuff, like whiskey. They're bunny lushes.

Number two: They can mimic human voices, and even throw their voices, although the one in my hamper hadn't said a word so far. (Number two was giving me real anxiety pangs, though, because the last thing I wanted was for that fuzzy lush to go around repeating my messages to Professor Twitchett. Especially message forty-two. I started hiccuping during that message, I was so worked up. Talk about embarrassing.)

Number three: They're shy, which seemed pretty okay to me.

And oh yeah, number four: They're ruthless killers. Which is just what you want to hear about your new roommate.

Apparently, jackalopes are cute and cuddly and shy and even friendly until you tick them off—then they go for the jugular with their slashy killer antlers. And judging from the state of my gym suit, they're pretty good at using them.

I stared at the hamper and considered my options. Which were pretty much nonexistent. I had to get in touch with Professor Twitchett.

I was dialing for the fifty-first time when my dad knocked on the door.

"Jeremy? Time for bed." He stuck his head inside just as I lurched to my feet.

"What? Great. Sure." I hoped he wouldn't look inside the hamper. If he looked inside the hamper I was dead. Or we both were, depending on how threatened Twitchett's experiment felt.

"What's this project you're working on?" Dad leaned against the door frame. He glanced around the room, probably expecting to see project-related papers or something. I bobbed nervously in front of the hamper.

"Just, you know. Science fair." I rolled my eyes. "I figured I'd do the planets, maybe? I've been coming up with ideas." I hoped that would cover the lack of any signs of productivity.

"That sounds good," Dad said, nodding. "I used to be an astronomy buff myself. Did you come up with something concrete?"

"Yeah, you know. Styrofoam."

Dad frowned slightly but nodded again. "Okay, we'll make that work. I can take you to get supplies after work tomorrow. Sound good?"

"Great!" I smiled and bobbed some more, hoping that bobbing in front of a jackalope wasn't like waving a red flag in front of a bull. My butt was feeling pretty exposed and vulnerable.

"Okay. Well, get some sleep, champ." Dad punched me on the shoulder. "Lights out."

I nodded. "Good night!" I closed the door behind him and sank to the floor.

It was true; the science fair was coming up. In two days, actually. And I know my dad was hoping I'd get a ribbon or something. And if you'd asked me yesterday, it would've been a pretty big priority. Not so big that I'd actually started on it yet, but big. And I definitely would've come up with something awesome, or at least awesomer than Styrofoam planets. But right now my main priority was just surviving until the fair.

The science fair had given me an idea, though. Wikipedia wasn't enough. I had to test my theory, make sure what I was dealing with.

I sat on the floor staring at my hamper until I heard my parents go to bed. Then I snuck out into the kitchen.

My dad always likes to get those tiny little airplane bottles of alcohol whenever he goes on trips, and he had a pretty good collection. I crept up to the shelf where he kept the bottles and poked around, trying to identify the whiskey ones. There was one right in front, but it had a bunch of red wax around the top, which made it pretty noticeable and probably messy to open, neither of which was good. It was too big a risk. I put it back into its little dust-free circle and kept poking around. Another one farther back looked pretty basic and plain, like it wouldn't be missed. And it was all in the name of science, right? I stuck it into my jeans pocket and snagged a Dixie cup from the bathroom before sneaking back into my room. It was time for the riskiest part of my plan.

I unscrewed the bottle top and poured the whiskey into the cup. Then I peered over the edge of the hamper.

The jackalope was hunkered down in what used to be my gym suit, glaring up at me with murder in his eyes. Or with a sleepy expression, one or the other. It's hard to say. I held the Dixie cup by the extreme edge and reached into the hamper, nestling the cup in the underwear fluff near the jackalope (but making sure to keep my fingers clear of the antler area). Then I waited.

The jackalope kept glaring at me for a couple of long minutes, and then its nose got to working. It sniffed at the air suspiciously and then heaved itself up onto its feet. It blinked its huge eyes at me and then hopped over to the cup. So far so good.

After one last suspicious look at me, it leaned forward and quickly lapped up the whiskey with a dainty

38

pink tongue. Then it sat back on its haunches, smacked its lips, and belched like a trucker.

It was an impressive display. A belch like that could win a guy some major points.

The jackalope burped again and flopped over onto its side, but I barely noticed. I slumped back against the wall, all the energy drained out of me. My experiment had worked. It was definitely a jackalope. Which meant one thing. I didn't care what Professor Twitchett said. I needed help.

I needed Agatha.

4.

I Convince a Girl to Go Out with Me

That must've been the longest night of my life. I don't think I slept at all. Even if the idea of a jackalope in my room hadn't kept me awake, the snoring would've. That mutant bunny practically stripped the paint off my walls, he was so loud.

I fished the shredded remains of Twitchett's note out of the hamper while the little monster slept, but the pieces that had survived didn't give me much to go on. My favorite shred, the biggest one, said *handsomely reward you for your troub*, which sounded fine to me. I could deal with a reward. The smaller shreds didn't sound as promising, though. I tried to put the note back together, but some key parts had definitely been ingested. All that was left in the end was *logize, but no choi, room is the only place they don't kno, grave danger from*, and *not what they seem*. Hardly a bedtime story, especially when you don't have any idea what isn't what it seems or what the danger is.

I did my best to think of any alternative to talking to Agatha, but I came up dry every time. I don't want to say hanging out with her is social suicide, but with her big mouth, she can clear a lunch table faster than anybody I know. (So yeah, it's social suicide.) But she knows Twitchett, she knows about science crap, and she wouldn't give me half the grief that Clint Warburton would if he found out I was freaked by a tiny mutant bunny. So it had to be Agatha. I just hoped Twitchett would get over it and give me the reward anyway.

So, no sleep? That was the downside. The upside was that I was dressed and ready to go by the time Mom and Dad were up for breakfast. And as tired as I was, I was definitely looking perkier than Mom.

"What's the matter? Are you okay?"

Mom's eyes were red and watery, and she had a pile of used tissues in the trash can next to her. She shrugged. "Allergies, I guess," she said.

"Your mom came into contact with something that really set her off," Dad said, padding over to the table with a glass of juice for her.

"That's too bad," I said, a frozen smile on my face. Because I knew exactly what must've set Mom off.

I told you about Killer, my rat with the pink eyes? Well, what I didn't tell you is that Killer was my rat for a grand total of maybe three days. That's how long it took for us to figure out that Mom was massively allergic and to find him a new home. He lives with Keisha Albright now, and answers to Sweetums. She brought in a picture of him last year. He was wearing a pink bow around his neck and posing in a Barbie Dream House. I don't like to talk about it.

If Mom can't handle a puny white rat like Killer, she definitely wouldn't be able to handle a freaking jackalope. I cussed at Professor Twitchett in my head and grabbed my jacket.

"I figured I'd better go in early. Do some research for my project."

Mom nodded, bleary-eyed, and waved me away as she staggered off into their bedroom, Dad following behind her with the box of tissues.

"Okay then. Bye!" I swung my backpack over my shoulder and headed for the door. I'd flushed Twitchett's note down the can, shut the jackalope up in my hamper again, and chucked the empty whiskey bottle into the Dumpster under my window—perfect shot, too. (The jackalope seemed to have eaten the Dixie cup.) The plan was to track Agatha down before school, ask her where Twitchett was, and get rid of that thing.

But, of course, plans change. Mine changed the minute I opened my door and came face to face with Mr. Jones.

I think I handled the situation well. I immediately slammed the door in his face and locked it. It was an impulse and I went with it. So sue me.

I leaned against the door and tried to figure out what to do. I knew I only had a minute or two, tops, before he wormed his way inside the apartment. And once he was inside again, it wasn't going to be easy to get rid of him. And I wasn't going to let him find that jackalope. Forget about the whole mythological creature thing—Mom would kill me if she thought I had a secret pet.

There was only one thing I could do. I rushed back into my bedroom and emptied my backpack onto the floor of the closet. Then I marched over to the hamper. I didn't even think about what I was about to do—I just did it. Which was good, because if I'd thought about actually touching that crazy antlered killer, I think I would've puked in my gym shoes.

Taking a deep breath, I opened the hamper, reached in, and had that puny jackalope around the middle before he'd even realized what I was doing. He squeaked and waggled his legs angrily, but thankfully he simmered down pretty quickly. Which was lucky for me, because it's not easy to act cool when your hand's a bloody stump.

I set the jackalope down carefully inside my backpack and slowly zipped it up, ready to jump back and out of the way if he went after me. But he didn't—he just eyed me angrily, probably plotting the best angle for jumping up and lopping off the top of my skull. Those antlers were a huge problem, too—they made a couple of nasty-looking holes in the backpack when I tugged on it a bit to get it shut. Not a good sign. I had just finished zipping it up (except for the new "breathing" holes in the top) when I heard Dad talking to Mr. Jones at the door.

I pressed myself up against the wall next to my door and peeked out, listening so hard my ears practically bled.

"I'm sorry, he's left for school already, but come inside, please." Dad ushered Mr. Jones into the living room. I ducked back so they wouldn't spot me. I don't know why I bothered, though, because Mr. Jones knew I was still here, and he was going to bust me any second now. I had one chance.

As soon as Mr. Jones was in the living room, I made my move, slipping out as quietly as I could. I eased the door shut behind me and stood motionless for a second, but no one came after me, so I don't think they'd noticed my stealthy moves.

I took off down the stairs, taking three at a time. I had to talk to Agatha. Everything would be fine once I talked to Agatha. Twitchett wouldn't like it, and her mom wouldn't be happy with me banging on the door so early, but that was just too bad.

But when I got to the bottom of the stairs, I stopped so fast I almost tripped over my feet. The other Upstairs Mr. Suit, aka Suit # 2, was standing in front of Agatha's door.

I have to admit, I just kind of stood there for a second (doing an unintentional Dewey impression) until that fruitcake Mrs. Simmons opened her door and beckoned to me. Mr. Suit #2 was watching me carefully, and that sure didn't seem like a good thing, so I gave her a friendly wave and hustled over. Which, if Mr. Suit #2 knew anything about me at all, was like waving a huge banner that said, "I'm up to something." Good thing he didn't know me.

Mrs. Simmons clutched at my shoulder and pulled me inside as she shut the door. She smelled like menthol and mothballs. Not a good combo.

"So many fine young men, Jerome! So many!" Mrs. Simmons smoothed her housedress and winked at me. "Are they here to see me?"

I just barely kept myself from rolling my eyes. Mrs. Simmons is such a fruit loop. I didn't even bother to correct her on my name. At least she got the first letter right this time. "I think they're looking for Professor Twitchett, Mrs. Simmons. The scientist? Upstairs?" My mind was going so fast it was hard to keep straight what she was saying. The more I thought about it, the more I realized Mr. Jones and his Suit sidekick didn't seem like cops, and they didn't really have a gangster vibe either. I felt my stomach lurch. They were probably a bigger deal, maybe Feds. FBI. Something like that.

"The scientist Twitchell? Where did he go?" Mrs. Simmons tugged on my arm so hard I thought my shirt would come off. I sighed and tried not to lose my cool, which is not easy when you're dealing with Mrs. Simmons. I think she did one of those sell-the-house-because-stairs-are-too-hard things old people are always doing, so I shouldn't blame her for being a total space case. But sheesh, there aren't that many people in the building. You'd think she could keep us straight.

Mrs. Simmons nodded. "What do they want? Who do they work for? Why do they want him? Do you think they'll come in for tea? I don't have any shortbread cookies." She wrung her hands nervously and looked at the door to the hallway.

I seriously doubted either Mr. Suit would be stopping in to chat with Mrs. Simmons, but I didn't want to be rude. I put on a thoughtful look and held my backpack farther away to keep it away from her clutchy hands. The last thing I needed was for her grabbiness to start a jackalope bloodbath.

"They probably won't have time, Mrs. Simmons. They say the Professor's inherited some money. They're from the bank, I guess." I rolled my shoulder. Mrs. Simmons may be old, but she's wiry, and I was pretty sure I was going to have a bruise where she'd been clutching me.

Mrs. Simmons shook her head. "Money. You don't believe that." She was watching me like a hawk. If she figured out that I thought they were Feds, she'd never let me leave. Either that or she'd pass out from excitement. I *so* didn't need this.

I shrugged. "You're right—it's probably something about an experiment. I've got to go now, okay?"

Mrs. Simmons nodded. "After you tell me about the experiment."

I sighed. "No, I can't, Mrs. Simmons. I have to go to school."

Mrs. Simmons wrung her hands so hard I could hear the bones popping. "You'll come back? You'll tell me what's happening? Agatha hasn't come home. I've been waiting and watching all night." She clutched at my shoulder again. Dang, that was definitely going to leave a mark. I pulled free.

"Yeah, sure. Agatha's not back yet?" My heart sank. She'd been gone all weekend, but I was counting on her being back by now.

"No, no Agatha," said Mrs. Simmons. "You'll come back? Tell me what they want?"

"Sure." I put the backpack back on gingerly and

peeked out of the door. The man was still there, but I put on my cool and casual attitude and sauntered past. "See you, Mrs. S!" I called over my shoulder, just to show how relaxed and unconcerned I was. Then I booked it as soon as I hit the pavement.

I found Agatha pretty much two seconds after I walked into school.

Just to warn you about Agatha—first off, we're not what you would call friends. We go to the same school and live in the same building, but that's the extent of it. Second, she's loud. And not exactly discreet. Which was going to pose a problem to a person with a top secret imaginary animal in his backpack. (That would be me.)

I followed the sound of Agatha's voice to her locker, where she was in the middle of a pissing match with Carter Oliver. (Not literally.) Those two have been numbers one and two in the science fair every year since third grade. Agatha's still got a huge chip on her shoulder about last year, because she thought she was going to win big with her working model of the *Titanic* (complete with real iceberg, sinking, and Celine Dion soundtrack). She didn't count on Carter's laser-operated garbage incinerator, though, and she's been bitter ever since. That, plus he incinerated her *Titanic* captain, making it impossible for him to go down with the ship.

So dealing with Agatha and Carter before I'd even eaten breakfast? This was really my lucky day.

Carter Oliver is this super smart, super good-looking, super athletic, all-around perfect person. Everybody loves him—teachers, kids, parents, chipmunks, you name it. If you met him, you'd think he was the best kid ever. Just being around him makes my hair get greasier, my face turn pimply, and my muscles all turn to flab instantly. Add that to the fact that I was publicly seeking out Agatha of all people, and socially, I was going to be a troll by the end of the day.

"Uh, Agatha?" I tugged on her sleeve. I wanted to make this quick.

Agatha jerked her arm away and, naturally, totally ignored me. "Fine, Carter. But if you think your stupid invisibility project is going to win, you're delusional.

My project is going to Blow. The. Judges. *Away*," she said, punctuating each word with a finger poke to Carter's chest.

Carter smiled a thousand-megawatt smile. Did I mention he'd done some modeling as a baby? "Hey, I just want a fair competition, Agatha. And since you aren't even willing to share what your project is . . ." He shrugged, like she was the lamest loser on the planet. (Which, normally, I wouldn't argue with, but it was Carter saying it, so I was torn.) Then he turned and sauntered off down the hall.

Agatha's face went another shade pinker, and I thought smoke was going to start coming out from under her collar. Fun to watch, but I didn't have time for it. "Uh, Agatha?"

"*What*?" She turned on me, shrieking. "What do *you* want?"

"You weren't at home this morning, and . . ."

"What do *you* care?" Agatha glared at me. "I stayed with my dad this weekend and he dropped me here. So what? Goldfish invisibility shield. *Ha*. Like that'll work."

I adjusted my backpack. I felt like I was carrying a bomb in there. Not a good feeling. "It's Professor Twitchett, okay? He's missing, and there are these men, and . . ."

Agatha snorted. "What, like I *care* what Twitchett does? He *banned* me, remember? I'm not allowed near his apartment or his precious lab."

She sure wasn't making this easy. I gave up trying to soft-pedal it. Besides, people were starting to stare. "Okay, I have to show you something. It's Twitchett's, okay?"

Agatha didn't seem the least bit interested. "I'm not interested," she said. See? That's how I could tell.

"No, you'll want to see this. Please? I need some advice here."

Another snort. "Forget it."

I played my ace. "Twitchett specifically told me not to tell you."

She rolled her eyes and flipped her hair over her shoulder. "Okay, fine. What is it?"

I glanced around the hallway. It was early, sure, but not that early. I didn't want to be waving a mythological beast around willy-nilly. "Come on. Outside."

Agatha folded her arms. "Oh, please."

"I'm serious, okay?" I grabbed Agatha and half-dragged her down the hallway, ducking my head down so nobody would recognize me. It's not like I wanted my name linked with hers for the rest of the year, okay?

I dragged her out of the side door and onto the loading dock of the school. I gritted my teeth. If Agatha wasn't willing to help me, I didn't know what I was going to do.

"Now brace yourself. Try not to freak out," I said, taking off my backpack. I had visions of hysterical screaming and crying, snot, the works.

She rolled her eyes again. "Give me a break. Just open the stupid backpack."

I unzipped the backpack and held it out to her. I probably should've made sure she was near a soft place in case she passed out, but it was too late for that now.

Agatha leaned forward and peeked into the backpack. "What is . . . is that . . ." She trailed off, her face going super pale and then so red I thought it would explode. Then she took a deep breath and shrieked. "THAT THIEF!"

5.

Agatha Improves My Vocabulary

Okay, that wasn't exactly the reaction I was expecting. My brain hadn't even worked out why Agatha was calling Twitchett a thief when she let loose with a stream of cusswords. Most of which I've only ever heard on late-night movies that I'm technically not even supposed to be watching.

"That scumsucker! What a *liar*!" Then she let another stream of impressive cusswords fly. I knew I had to move fast. Nothing gets the teachers running faster than what they like to call "detention words." And seriously, I don't even think the words Agatha was using qualified as detention words. More like "expelled from school and put into juvie indefinitely" words. (I did make a mental note to write some of them down later, though. Because honestly? Genius. I was just itching to unleash those beauties next time Nick Hurley elbowed me going for a basket.)

I grabbed Agatha the potty mouth by the arm again and dragged her across the pavement and behind a tree near the bleachers. Confession time—I don't have a lot of experience dealing with cussing girls. There had to be a way to shut the floodgates, but I wasn't seeing it. There must be a trick to it.

"Agatha, cut it out, okay? You're not helping!" I wasn't about to wait her out, either. She was insulting her way through Twitchett's entire family line, and the girl knows her genealogy.

Agatha turned on me. "You don't understand. That's *mine*, okay? *Mine*."

"Fine, it's yours!" Believe me, if she wanted to take the jackalope problem off my hands, I wasn't going to stop her. "He probably missed you. Here you go."

I held out the backpack, but Agatha stared at me like I'd just farted in the punch bowl.

"No, nitwit, not the rabbit. The rabbit isn't mine. The *idea*. I had *notes*." She rolled her eyes and flopped down on the lowest bleacher seat.

I sat down next to her. It was all clear to me now. She didn't understand.

"No, Agatha," I started, trying not to sound too condescending. "This isn't a rabbit, okay? Normal rabbits don't have antlers. This," I took a dramatic breath, "is a jackalope."

Agatha gave me that punch bowl look again. "No, loser, that's a rabbit. Or, technically, a rabbit hybrid. Chimera, if you want to get really fancy, except only in the genetic sense of the word, not the classical."

I set my jaw. I'd read my Wikipedia. I knew a jackalope when I saw one. "No, it's a jackalope. See the antlers?"

Agatha rolled her eyes again. "It's an animal hybrid, and I know, because *I'm* the one who had the idea. *I'm* the one who did the research and figured out how we could create a jackalope look-alike in the lab. *I'm* the one who suggested using my rabbit's genetic material as a base.

I'm the one who recommended axis deer DNA instead of antelope for more traditional antlers. And *I'm* the one who planned to present the jackalope *as my science fair project.*"

I opened my mouth and shut it again. Because one, I didn't understand half of that, and two, if the part I did understand was true, I'd be ticked, too. A jackalope would beat a goldfish with an invisibility shield any day of the week. Even if it was just a hybrid whatever.

"So why was he in my bed?" I cut to the chase.

Agatha gave a huge sigh. "Because *Twitchett* wouldn't let me do it. *Twitchett* said it wouldn't work. That even if it would, it was immoral and unethical and I was too immature to recognize my limitations. And *Twitchett* had 'grave doubts about my scientific integrity and entire system of ethics' and *banned* me. Apparently, so he could steal my ideas! He's a washed-up thieving loser hack."

Wow, sucks to be Agatha. (Still didn't really explain the bed part, though.)

I didn't have a chance to say that though, because Agatha took a deep breath and went into a new rant. I scooched a little farther away from her. She was really going at it with the air quotes, and I didn't want to lose an eye. "I asked him to harvest Hortense's eggs for the project. Not a lot, okay? Just a couple. And you know what he did? He told my parents about my 'ethical disorder,' and they had her spayed! *He fixed my rabbit.*" Agatha went off on another cussing jag, under her breath this time.

I'd kind of forgotten about Hortense, Agatha's rabbit, but now that she mentioned it, the jackalope did look a little like Hortense around the fangs. Which, believe me, wasn't a good thing, since Hortense was the nastiest rabbit known to mankind.

I peered into my backpack to get a better look at the jackalope/animal hybrid/whatever. It was looking pretty ticked off, nothing unusual there, and it was eyeing the opening like it was thinking of making a break for it. I didn't blame it—Agatha's ranting was enough to make anyone want to head for the hills. (I sure did.)

I was trying to figure out how to zip the backpack again without losing a finger when I noticed that the cussing seemed to have stopped. Pretty abruptly, too. I shot a side look at Agatha, and she actually looked like she'd cheered up. I shook my head. I don't understand moody chicks, and that was the fastest mood change I'd ever seen. That should have tipped me off, but for some reason I didn't realize that cheery Agatha equals trouble.

"That really stinks about Twitchett," I said cautiously. "But what are we going to about this guy?" I nodded toward the bag.

Agatha gave me a huge scary smile. "Oh, don't worry about him. He's fine."

"Really?" I didn't see how he could be fine. "How is he fine?"

Agatha smiled bigger. "He's my new science fair project."

I jerked the bag back so fast that the jackalope barked angrily, whipped his head out, and slashed one of the straps with his antlers. "Forget it." Giving the jackalope back to his rightful owner was one thing, but I wasn't going to stand by and watch Agatha trot him out to be gawked at. I don't have much experience with the furry set, but I know Killer would've hated that. More than he must hate that stinking bow Keisha's always dressing him up in. (Not that I've asked, okay? I'm over it.)

Besides, Twitchett said I had a reward coming, and she wasn't going to screw me out of that.

Agatha shot out a skinny arm and grabbed the loose strap, tugging it back toward her. "Give it."

"Oh, no," I said, trying not to get into a tug-of-war with her. "You can't do that, Agatha."

"Why not?" She gritted her teeth and pulled harder. "It's my idea, my work. I've got most of my calculations—I'll just re-create my notes. Carter can eat my dust."

"But you can't!" I pulled back and tried to think of a convincing argument. You know, besides the "You've gone psycho crazy" argument. "You've already got a great project. What about the idea you're working on now?"

Agatha stopped tugging. "What idea?"

"You know, the one that's going to beat the invisible goldfish?" I said lamely. It would've been a more convincing argument if I actually knew what her project was.

Agatha gave a short, scary laugh. "You want to know what my idea is? Do you?"

Believe me, I didn't want to nod. But I did.

"I don't have an idea, okay? I have no project. I've got less than twenty-four hours to beat the socks off of Carter Oliver and I've got *nothing.*"

I made a sympathetic face. My lame planets idea suddenly seemed pretty okay. At least it was better than nothing.

"My parents don't want to let me around anything remotely scientific because, thanks to Twitchett, they're afraid I'm going unleash deadly bacteria on the world or blow up the neighborhood with my chemistry set. They want me to make electricity with a potato."

I understood. Electricity with a potato is cool, but we did that in class a couple of years ago. Even I knew she couldn't do electricity with a potato.

"Well, that sucks," I said in my most sympathetic voice. "But you still can't have the jackalope." I jerked the backpack strap out of her hand and zipped it up so quickly that I almost amputated a jackalope nose in the process.

"Animal hybrid! Not jackalope!" Agatha shrieked. "But why? What difference does it make if he's my project? What do you care?"

I didn't answer. I'd just seen something through the spaces in the bleachers that made my stomach drop. I dropped to the ground to get a better look.

"What are you doing?" Agatha stared at me.

I couldn't believe it. We were in big trouble. "That's why," I said, pointing.

Two long black cars had pulled up next to the school.

6.

My Secret Life Revealed

"No way," Agatha said, peering through the hedges at the school. We'd ditched the bleachers for some nearby bushes that were less exposed. "It doesn't make any sense. Why would the Suits care about us? Unless you let them see the rabbit hybrid. Did you? Just admit it."

I'd filled Agatha in on all the Mr. Suit activities at our apartment, but apparently she still thought I was a doofus. "Yeah, I introduced them first off. Sheesh, what do you think, I'm an idiot?"

"Fine, sorry. But why us, then? We don't know where Twitchett is. We're just a couple of stupid kids." Agatha shook her head.

"Hey!"

"Well, to *them*! They shouldn't be paying any attention to us at all."

She had a point. If I were looking for Twitchett, I don't think I'd be wasting my time stalking a couple of kids who can't even drive yet. They must have security cameras to check or phones to tap or something, right?

"Who are they anyway? Cops?"

I shook my head. "Feds. Have to be, right? Maybe FBI. Or CIA." I went cold just thinking about it. Those CIA guys could eat you for lunch. I've seen the movies.

Agatha stood up. "Come on. We're going back in."

I grabbed her and tried to drag her back down into a crouch. "What, are you crazy? They'll see you! I said CIA, Agatha!"

Agatha pulled her arm loose. "Your scenario doesn't make sense, Jeremy. According to you, they shouldn't even know you were helping Twitchett. Sorry, but there's got to be a logical explanation. Let's find out what it is."

I trotted after her (keeping my head ducked down) as she walked casually back toward the school. "But . . ."

Agatha shot a scornful look back at me. "Relax, they're not going to hurt a couple of kids. And I'm not going to be an idiot about it. Like some people."

Yeah, put-downs were really what I needed. That's the thanks I get for trying to be a good guy. We got to the back entrance of the school, but the whole way I was sure that any second now, guys in suits were going to jump me from behind.

Tori Bartholomew was jogging out of the door as we came up. Agatha shot a hand out and grabbed her by the arm as she hurried past, jerking her back like a rag doll.

"Hey, Tori, what's up?" Agatha flipped her hair over her shoulder, all casual, like she hadn't just jerked Tori's arm half out of the socket.

Tori scowled at her, rubbed her arm, and pulled her tights up. Very attractive move, the hitching up of the tights. Just a shade more attractive than the wiping of the nose.

"Oh, they were making an announcement for you. Your uncle's here to pick you up? You need to go to the office." Tori finished fiddling with her tights and swung her backpack over her shoulder.

"My uncle?" Agatha raised an eyebrow and shot me a significant look.

"Yeah, that's what they said, so look, I gotta go," Tori said in one breath. "Oh, your uncle too, Jeremy. What, are you related?" She gave her tights one last tug and hurried off around the building without waiting for an answer.

Agatha folded her arms and looked thoughtful.

"Let me guess. No uncle?"

Agatha shook her head. "Not that I know of. You?"

Nothing like a little validation to make your day. "Nope. And what does that tell you?" I bragged.

"That I need more information." Agatha glared at me and stalked into the building, maybe a little bit more slowly than before.

I have to say, I did notice that people were staring at us as we walked through the hall, but I thought it was because I was with Agatha. (Or because they thought we were related, which really, I don't even want to think about.) I didn't realize that it was because I'd been pegged as a criminal fugitive from justice. I didn't figure that out for a whole two minutes more, when I saw the Mr. Suit types searching my locker. They were at Agatha's, too.

I half-expected Agatha to explode and go beat them up for daring to touch her Einstein pinups, but she didn't; she just hung back and gaped. I think she finally realized maybe I wasn't as brain-dead as she thought.

To be fair, I was doing my own fair share of gaping when Nick Hurley punched me on the shoulder. "Way to go, man. What'd you do?"

I shrugged. "Nothing much." I jerked my head at the Suits. "What've you heard?" I have to admit, as bad as things were, I was pretty psyched. This jackalope thing could be just what I needed to ramp up my rep.

"That they're the Feds and that you guys are arms dealers. Also, that you're on the run for embezzling money from the Mob. Or that your uncles are staging an intervention and searching your lockers for drugs." Nick grinned. "Nobody has a clue, so you're in the clear. But nobody believes those guys are your uncles."

I nodded. That uncle story was pretty lame. Especially since they were using the same story for me and Agatha. I had to hand it to them, though—it was a sneaky way to get access to our lockers. Principal Turner's so freaked out about alienating parents and family members that she would've opened our lockers for the family dog.

"I'd clear out if I were you, though," Nick said, keeping an eye on the locker situation. "They'll be done there soon, and they'll find you. But me? I never saw you." He punched me again and headed off down the hallway.

I nudged Agatha, who was still staring slack-jawed at the Suits. "Look," she whispered.

One of the Suits had the shrimpy kid whose locker was next to Agatha's by the upper arm and was whispering in his ear in a really creepy, no-concept-of-personal-space kind of way. When the kid shook his head, the Suit pressed on the kid's neck for a second and he slumped against the wall like his bones had gone to jelly. It was just for a second, and I wouldn't even have noticed if I hadn't been looking right at them. Then the kid kind of straightened up, and when the Suit asked him something else, he nodded.

"He's done that three times now," Agatha whispered. "Who are these guys?"

"Beats me." That didn't look like a CIA move. That looked like a Vulcan nerve pinch, like on *Star Trek*. I didn't even want to think what that meant. "We've got to get out of here."

Agatha snapped her jaw shut and nodded. "Right. But first things first." She narrowed her eyes and got a scary focused expression on her face. It was like she'd woken up from a coma. "Do you have a cell phone?" She held out her hand, and when I was too slow, started snapping her fingers. "Come on! Come on! Cell phone!"

"Okay! Fine!" I handed over my phone.

"They can track us with these, you know," Agatha said. "So first thing we do is destroy them."

"Hey!" I snatched my phone back. "I don't think so."

Agatha rolled her eyes. "Fine, we hide them. But we can't take them with us."

We decided that the best place for the phones was the dusty dead-bug area under the stairs. And I knew she was right—I'd read all about GPS stuff. But I still had a twinge when I turned my phone off and stashed it in the grime.

"Now let's get going."

"Great. Where?" I fiddled with the slashed strap of my backpack. As fun as this all was, it was important to remember that I was going around with a killer strapped to my back. And I can't say I had a lot of faith in Agatha's plan, no matter what it was. I mean, one more slash and I'd be carrying the jackalope in my pocket.

"Twitchett." Agatha adjusted her bag.

Yeah, great plan, wish I'd thought of it. "Twitchett. Right. Where is he again?"

Agatha smirked. "Trust me."

Great. But it's not like I had a lot of other options.

We dodged Mr. Burgess, the hall monitor, and hightailed it out of the school just as the bell rang. The parking lot was pretty dead except for this white van driving around, so it wasn't that hard to run between the cars without anyone spotting us. The Suits weren't guarding the doors or anything, so that was good. I don't know what we would've done if they had been. Forget the jackalope: I didn't want to end up handcuffed in a dirty cell somewhere with someone shining a light in my eyes.

We took off running, and you have to hand it to Agatha—she's good with her evasive maneuvers. The route we took was so confusing, I wasn't even sure where we were headed until I saw the giraffe waggling her tongue at me up ahead. "The zoo?" I squealed, and yes, my voice did crack a bit. But it was just from the shock. I mean, come on. And she called me an idiot? "Why would Twitchett be at the zoo? It'll be crawling with Suit guys, don't you think?"

Agatha didn't even bother to look back at me. She was really booking it. "It's worth a shot. And even if Twitchett's not there, Bob will be. And Bob's great."

Terrific. Like I even knew who Bob was.

Bob, apparently, was Professor Twitchett's assistant. Or at least, that's what Agatha told me as we peered through the window of Twitchett's lab building. Something I probably would know if I'd ever been to Twitchett's lab.

"So where's Bob?" I asked after we'd scanned the room for the millionth time. So far we hadn't seen any sign of Bob or any Mr. Suits or anything.

"Weird. He's not here," Agatha said. "I say we make our move anyway. Check out the office."

Agatha didn't wait for me to answer. She had a hairpin out and was picking the lock on the door before I even had a chance to protest. And once someone is picking a lock, there's not a lot you can do except stand in front of them to block them from view and whistle. (Well, that's what I do. Whistling is probably optional.)

"Got it!" Agatha said, scooting inside and dragging me along behind her. Those fourth-grade criminal habits were really paying off.

Inside it was what you'd call your basic lab. You know: It smelled funny, had Bunsen burners, lots of Pyrex, and sciencey junk. Beats me what we were looking for, but Agatha was going to town looking through papers and cabinets and stuff. I fiddled with a nasty-looking petri dish and waited for her to get done.

Agatha slammed down a pile of papers she'd been shuffling through and snorted in disgust. "Nothing here. Nothing interesting anyway, unless you're tracking hippo cholesterol levels."

Which, obviously, I wasn't.

Agatha eyed the petri dish I was holding. "That's bubonic plague, you know. Did you get it on your hand? Because if you did, you're going to break out in huge black boils and die."

I dropped the petri dish as Agatha burst out laughing. "It's not the plague, you dork," she gasped between very unattractive snorty laughs.

"I know," I said, pushing the petri dish away quickly and wiping my hands on my jeans. "What is it?"

Agatha wiped her eyes. "Like I know." She tested the inner door of the lab and then whipped out her hairpin again. "We'd better hurry and check out Twitchett's office before Bob comes back."

She messed with the lock for a few minutes before it clicked and she swung the door open. Then she stared in shock.

I didn't blame her. I think I've mentioned Twitchett's not exactly the most tidy person on the planet. His apartment has a lot in common with a nuclear waste dump. So when that door opened, I never would've believed it was Twitchett's office. It wasn't just that it was tidy. It was more than tidy. It had been cleaned out.

7.

Good Housekeeping Ruins Our Day

Agatha looked into the room and went into shock. "Nooo!" she wailed, rushing into the office. "Where are the papers? Where are the notes?"

She pulled file folders out of the racks that lined the walls, but they were all empty, except for a few stray paper clips here and there. "This doesn't make sense! Professor Twitchett kept notes on everything!"

"Maybe he took them with him?"

"Well, yeah, but . . . I mean . . ." Agatha looked around in desperation.

"Maybe he didn't want anyone to find them?" Seemed logical to me. I hadn't really expected to find a file with "Top Secret Jackalope Project" written across the front.

"Yes, I realize that, brainiac," Agatha said. "But look around. This wasn't a rush situation. Was he planning to leave? Because this took time, taking all of these papers out."

She had a point. The pens were lined up neatly beside the desk blotter. The file cabinets were all shut. Believe me, that kind of thing doesn't just happen.

Agatha stared around the room helplessly. "I thought there would be something, some clue about where he'd gone. A notepad or a file on the desk or something."

The jackalope squirmed in my backpack. He'd been getting kind of restless back there since we left the school, and I was starting to get worried. All that wailing was getting to him. And deep, gaping flesh wounds are hard to cover up.

"Maybe it wasn't him." I hated to say it flat out like that, but come on, Twitchett would never line up pens.

"Maybe it wasn't him." Agatha echoed sadly. She must've noticed the pens too.

"So, what now?" I slipped the backpack off of my back slowly. Just to get it a little farther away from my jugular.

Agatha nodded at the backpack. "He left the animal hybrid. He must be planning to come back."

No duh, since he pretty much said that in his note. "Well, good. I just wish he'd hustle." The jackalope gave a big kick and shook the backpack in my hand, like he was trying to bust his way out of a cocoon. "The faster the better." Twitchett was just lucky Mr. Jones had turned out to be such a jerk—if he'd been an okay guy I would've handed over the jackalope in a heartbeat, reward or no reward. Twitchett was so not worth all this trouble.

A shadow passed across the window and we heard someone whistling outside. "Bob!" Agatha said. "He'll know where Twitchett is!"

She shoved me out into the lab area and slammed the door to Twitchett's office just as Bob unlocked the lab door.

Bob turned out to be this skinny, frizzy-haired guy wearing a faded Slayer T-shirt. He had these watery blue eyes behind a pair of black hipster glasses and was holding a fancy camera. Everything about him screamed "trying to be cool." Basically, the kind of skeezy creep I do my best to avoid. I'm not a total Neanderthal, though. I can be polite. I stuck my hand out to introduce myself. "So you're Bob? I'm—"

"Agatha?" Bob interrupted, in this reedy voice that would've made me snicker any other day. He pushed past me, totally dissing my attempt to be cordial. "What are you doing here? You're banned, remember?"

Agatha shrugged. "Well, yeah, but, Professor Twitchett? He hasn't been around, and I thought . . . so where is he?"

Bob put his satchel down on the lab table and glanced around nervously. "I think he made himself pretty clear."

"Don't you know where he is?" Agatha blinked up at him with big puppy eyes. No one can resist that.

Bob shook his head. "Yeah, it's funny. I don't. Some guys were looking for him. But I'm sure he'll be back soon."

Yeah, right, Bob. Way to lie, buddy. His Adam's apple was bobbing around like it was Halloween.

Bob held up the camera apologetically and then shoved it into a drawer behind him. "Polar bear photos. Gotta keep up to date, you know." He laughed awkwardly. Like we cared what he'd been taking photos of. "Anybody want a soda? Jeremy? Agatha?"

Agatha shook her head. "We're pretty worried. And we need to talk to him about . . ."

I kicked Agatha in the shin, hard. I didn't even try to be subtle.

Agatha glared at me, but she got the point. "A project. Just an idea I had."

Bob's watery eyes widened "An idea you had? Oh, the—" He coughed, then reached out and tousled Agatha's hair. "What do you mean, something for school? You've got some big project? Maybe I could help."

Agatha laughed and ducked her head away. She was acting jokey, but come on, no one over the age of five wants their hair tousled. What does Bob think, we're preschoolers? "No, it's okay, I just need to talk to Twitchett."

"Yeah, well, that makes two of us. He's been super secretive lately, doesn't share a thing. Not since he won that award for inventing that baboon posterior salve. Just top secret this, top secret that, right?" Bob grinned and stared at Agatha a little too long. There was some weird tension in the air, but I couldn't put my finger on it, exactly. "Bet Jeremy knows all about it, though, right, Jeremy?"

He laughed again.

I shrugged. I was still trying to get over the baboon bomb Bob had just dropped. Posterior salve? Man, Agatha was right. Twitchett was a thief.

"Right?" Bob's beady eyes were still fixated on me. Apparently Bob didn't realize that sometimes a shrug is the only answer you get.

I rolled my eyes. "Beats me. Bubonic plague?"

Bob gave me a confused look, but Agatha grabbed me by the arm. "Yeah, thanks, Bob. You'll let me know if you hear from him?"

Bob nodded. I didn't like the way he was watching us, though. And something about the conversation was making all of my red flags shoot up, but I wasn't sure what. It wasn't just that Bob made me want to take a shower. I just wanted to get out of there. I slung my backpack over my shoulder, and that was when I heard the small ripping sound.

Agatha heard it, too, and a panicked expression shot across her face. Not exactly the look you want when you're trying to play things cool.

"Agatha, Jeremy, wait a minute," Bob said, taking a step toward us. "What's going on? You're not in school. What are you up to." He didn't even bother to make it a question, he just accused us flat out. Uncool, man.

Agatha smiled, "Conference day, that's all. Right, Jeremy?"

I nodded and shifted my weight nervously. The fabric on the backpack started to give way. Not much, maybe an inch. But enough to make me want to throw up. And enough to make Bob eye my bag suspiciously.

It's not like he was buying the conference stuff either. He narrowed his eyes. "Don't try to con me, Agatha. What have you got there?"

Agatha grabbed my arm. "Nothing! Thanks for the help! See you soon!" Then she made a break for the door.

I took off after her and felt the backpack rip again. I swung it around and clutched it to my chest just as the strap broke. I could feel the pointy prongs stabbing into my chest as I ran, but I didn't stop. I just hoped my grave-stone didn't end up saying "death by jackalope."

Thankfully, Bob didn't follow us. I'm guessing he has an allergy to anything that might be labeled "physical activity." He just watched through the window as we took off through the zoo and out into the park.

As soon as we were out of sight, Agatha gasped and flopped to the ground under a tree. "That was so stupid. All we did was make Bob suspicious. And he's a good guy! I'm so paranoid now! Why am I so paranoid of everybody?"

I shrugged and clutched nervously at the bag on my chest. Good guy or not, Bob creeped me out. But to be honest, everybody was creeping me out these days. And Bob was really the least of my concerns. I had the jackalope immobilized for the time being, but if he wanted to get free, I wasn't going to be able to stop him. He was one twitch away from a starring role on the ten o'clock news.

"Agatha, we've got a big problem here." I indicated the bag with my head.

"We've got a couple of big problems here," Agatha said, barely glancing at the bag. The jackalope squirmed and popped his head out of the top of my backpack. He looked like a jackalope burrito. So much for hiding him.

"Jeremy, we can't keep this up. Those guys in the suits? If they really are CIA, that's huge. We can't keep running from them. We've got to confront our problems head-on."

I nodded. "Great. Um, could you look at my bag a sec? Speaking of head-on?"

Agatha looked up and saw the jackalope staring down at her. "Oh, crap, Jeremy, you're supposed to keep him hidden."

"Yeah, sorry about that." Like the burrito look was my idea.

Agatha dug around in her book bag and pulled out a scarf, which she wrapped around the jackalope's head, so instead of a jackalope burrito, it looked like a turban-wearing bunny burrito. Much better.

"There's only one thing to do, Jeremy," she said, tying off the top of the turban.

"Oh yeah? What's that?" Since all of Agatha's ideas had turned out so well.

"We're going home. We're going to clear our names."

8.

I Play Keep-Away

"I don't know about this, Agatha." We were standing in the hedges of the apartment building across the street from ours. I was spending way too much time in hedges these days, that's for dang sure.

The jackalope was now safely stowed in an environmentally friendly reusable grocery bag made from all-recycled materials. (I know this because it was written in huge hot pink letters across the front of the bag. Pretty snazzy, if you're blind.) Agatha had picked it up at the local minimart on the way home. I owe her a dollar.

"Look, I know it seems dumb. But those Suits think we're involved, so they're not going to let up.

They've already cost me my perfect attendance medal for the year—I'm not letting them ruin anything else." Agatha's eyes were dark and crazy looking. I'm just glad she was blaming them for making her skip school instead of me.

"It's simple, okay?" Agatha hitched her bookbag up on her shoulder. "We do it one at a time, so if anything goes wrong, the other one can go for help. We keep the animal hybrid out of sight at all times. Once we've answered their questions, they'll realize we don't know anything and leave us alone, right?" Agatha looked like she'd convinced herself, at least.

I hoped she was right. I wasn't willing to live under surveillance for the next thirty years because my crazy neighbor left a mutant bunny in my bed.

We crept up to the front of the building and peered in. Agatha swore under her breath. "That stupid man in the suit is still there, just waiting for us. Jerk," she said. Not a big surprise, really. Once we'd ditched them at school, they had to figure we'd come back. After all, we do live there.

"Uh-oh. Trouble," I said. A large black car had turned the corner up ahead and was driving slowly down the street toward us. It looked a lot like the one that had shown up at school. Close enough that I wasn't going to risk hanging around.

We were totally stuck. We couldn't go inside and we couldn't stay outside. There weren't a lot of options. Those CIA/Vulcan/secret agent types sure know their stuff.

"Quick," Agatha said, cracking the door. "Maybe we can sneak past."

Right. The lobby is not that big. It'd be like sneaking past someone in the bathroom. They're going to notice. But we were just about to sneak inside anyway when we heard it.

"You! Hey, you! Up here!"

Mr. Suit #2 looked up and around. "Who's there?" he called suspiciously.

"Quick! There he goes! Over there! Come quick!" The voice sounded like it was coming from upstairs.

Mr. Suit #2 hesitated and then hurried up the stairs. I shot Agatha a surprised look. I didn't know who that was, but the distraction was just what we'd needed.

"You know what to do!" Agatha said, pushing me toward Mrs. Simmons' apartment.

I knocked lightly on the door, nervously eyeing the stairs.

Mrs. Simmons must have practically had her ear to the door, because she jerked it open immediately. "Jeffrey!"

"Mrs. Simmons! Hi, can I come in? Thanks." I winked at Agatha as I pushed my way past Mrs. Simmons into the apartment and ducked out of sight. Agatha nodded and started rattling her keys.

"Boy, it's good to be home!" she shouted, as Mr. Suit #2 came clattering down the stairs. Plan One in place. I peeked through the crack in the door.

"Excuse me, miss, I need to ask you a few questions."

Agatha turned around with her most innocent face on. Good thing, too, because Mr. Suit #2 looked really ticked off.

"I don't know what you're trying to pull, but this is a serious situation." Mr. Suit #2 didn't look like someone you want to mess with. I sure hoped Agatha's plan would work.

I scanned the hallway quickly as Mrs. Simmons closed the door. Funny, I didn't see whoever had called him away. I frowned and looked down at the eyes glinting at me from inside the environmentally friendly grocery bag.

"Is that a present for me?" Mrs. Simmons stood in front of the door and pointed at the bag. Weird how this part of the plan hadn't seemed quite so bad when we'd been talking about it. I must've been delusional.

"Uh, no, it's my uh . . . project. But you can have the bag later, if you want," I stammered, tucking the bag behind me. I could feel the jackalope peeking over the top. I just hoped its turban was still on tight.

"I'll just take that for you. It's for me, right? A present? A present because you didn't find out where Professor Twitchell went?" Mrs. Simmons reached around for the bag, and I held it farther back. Seriously, who's grabby like that? Except for five-year-olds, and it's not like they're even real people yet.

"No, I just haven't heard anything. He's not at the lab." I took a couple of steps back, but Mrs. Simmons isn't one of those people with a real good perception of personal space.

"Interesting." Mrs. Simmons was peering around my back at the bag. "Is that a doggie? I'll take that doggie."

I nodded. "Yes, that's it, it's a dog. For my project. I have to keep it in the bag though. That's my science project, Dog in a Bag. You don't mind if I keep it here for a little bit?"

Mrs. Simmons clasped her hands together tightly. "Oh, not at all. I like dogs. You can leave it here as long as you want. I'll take very good care of it. *Very* good care of it."

She smiled at me, showing all of her big horsey teeth.

"Great, I'm sure you would." No way in hell was I going to leave Jack alone with Mrs. Simmons. Crazed killer or not, that's just not something I would inflict on anyone. Mrs. Simmons, that is.

I spent the next million years alternately playing keep-away with Mrs. Simmons and cussing out Agatha in my head. Because hiding in Mrs. Simmons' apartment was supposed to be the easy part of the plan. It was the questioning part that we'd been nervous about.

Just when Mrs. Simmons had me ready to give myself up to the cops, Agatha crept into the apartment dragging a pink Dora the Explorer suitcase behind her.

"You okay?" I said, going over as she shut the door quietly behind her.

"Yes, but there's not much time," she whispered. "You've got a guard at your door, too, and mine's gone upstairs to consult. You better hustle. But first give me the hybrid."

"Jeffrey has a dog," Mrs. Simmons said loudly. "He's going to give him to me. He's my dog."

"Uh, no, Mrs. Simmons," I said. I couldn't help but smirk at the suitcase. "You going on the run, Agatha? With Dora?" I snickered.

"It's old, okay? From when I was little. And it's not for me, it's for the animal hybrid. You'll need your back-pack. For cover." She rolled her eyes at me.

She had a point.

It wasn't easy making the transfer, in part because we had to do it without getting our limbs ripped off by an angry turban-wearing burrito, and in part because we had to do it without Mrs. Noseypants Simmons noticing that my doggie was less than doggielike. (Which meant there was a little more dumping involved than I would've liked.) But seriously, from the minute Agatha said "animal hybrid," it was like she was all ears.

"I thought you said your project was Dog in a Bag. That looks like Dog in a Suitcase." One sharp cookie, that Mrs. Simmons. Can't put anything past her.

"That's part two of my project."

"We're studying how he adjusts to different environments, right?" Agatha shot me a look. "It's a comparative study. He was in a cardboard box earlier."

I cleared my throat. "That's right."

"I see." Mrs. Simmons raised her eyebrows thoughtfully. Score one for Agatha.

I zipped the suitcase shut. I have to admit, I felt kind of weird leaving him with Agatha. It's not like that bunny stinker was anything but a pain in my neck, but it felt strange to just leave him behind. But I shook it off, grabbed the shreds of my backpack, and hurried into the hallway. I was just in time. Mr. Suit #2 was coming back down the stairs as I was going up.

I hardly glanced at him as I brushed past. But I was so busy being cool and casual that I didn't even see Mrs. Garcia coming around the corner. Or stop before she bumped into my arm. And knocked my backpack onto the floor.

"Oh, Jeremy! I'm so sorry! Here, let me . . . what's this?"

My experience with Mrs. Garcia has pretty much been limited to accepting cookies, so I didn't realize how quick she could be. I barely had time to react before she bent over and picked up my backpack and then stood there looking at it, not giving it back right away like a normal person would. After a minute, she looked up at me, and I didn't like the look on her face. It was that super sympathetic look that teachers give you right before they ask you if there's something you want to tell them.

"Wow, Jeremy, this looks like it's taken quite a beating." She stuck her fingers through the slash marks in the top. "What happened here?"

"Oh, that? Nothing," I said. I figured denial was the best way to go. What did she care anyway, right? It's not like it was her backpack.

"Did something cut this? It looks like it was cut with something sharp." Mrs. Garcia cocked her head and looked at me intently. "Is there something you'd like to talk about?"

Great. The teacher question. I shook my head.

"Did someone do this to your bag? One of your classmates?"

I shrugged. "It's just messed up, that's all. Bad quality."

"And where are your books?" Man, Mrs. Garcia was not letting this go. It was just a stupid backpack. I don't know why she was giving me the third degree.

"At school. Look, sorry I wasn't paying attention." I snatched the backpack out of her hand and hurried toward my apartment. She was still staring me like I was a homeless puppy or something when I got to the door.

I turned my back on her and concentrated on the lock. Mrs. Garcia didn't matter. I had bigger problems right now.

Mr. Jones was waiting.

9.

Agatha Gets a Makeover

"Just tell the truth, Jeremy. We know you're lying."

Agatha's idea to clear our names? Not one of the top ten ideas of all time. Probably would've been better if we'd done it when our parents were home. Just to protect our constitutional rights and keep us from getting grilled within an inch of our lives, you know, that kind of thing. Not to mention avoiding the preliminary patdown. That was a joy, believe me. All that was missing was the blinding light shining in my eyes and the rickety folding chair.

"We have evidence that you were involved with Professor Twitchett's experiments, Jeremy. Or should I say Igor? You're an intelligent boy. Tell us where he is."

I wished I had chosen one of the stiff chairs in the living room instead of the couch. There's no way to look dignified under questioning when you've sunk a good six inches into the cushions. Mr. Jones was obviously pretty experienced—he'd chosen a hard chair that was just perfect for looming over me.

"Look, I don't know, okay? I told you. I went by the lab, but he wasn't there. If he's not there and he's not home, I don't know." I put my head in my hands.

Mr. Jones smiled. "But you know what he was working on. Don't you? You have it. Or you know where it is."

"Who are you guys, anyway? CIA? FBI? Homeland Security, something like that?"

Mr. Jones just smiled his creepy smile. So it looked like three strikes for me.

"It's time to come clean. You're not fooling anyone."

I stood up. "Look. Search me again. Search my room again. Call your goons back and search wherever you want, okay? I don't have anything, I don't know anything. I didn't do any experiment. I got a C− in science last term. Just leave me alone."

Mr. Jones folded his arms. "All you need to do is answer two questions. What was Professor Twitchett working on, and where did he go? Two little answers and we'll go away. Then it won't even matter who we are."

Taking a deep breath, I looked Mr. Jones straight in the eye. Grown-ups seem to be big on that. "Look, I'm just his gofer. I got him some Preparation H once, okay? For some baboon butt salve he won some big prize for. That's it—that's all I know. I didn't know I was doing anything illegal. But Twitchett, he couldn't invent his way out of a paper bag."

"The truth, Jeremy."

I swallowed hard and looked at my sneakers. We'd gone through the same set of questions over and over, which I guess is some kind of interrogation technique to make you mess up your answers. But that was easy—all I had to do was pretend the past twenty-four hours hadn't happened, which, believe me, I really wished they hadn't. And when you know that one slipup means that a jerkwad like Jones wins, it makes it that much easier to lie.

The hardest part was watching as I don't know how many agents went through our house, which Mom probably would not have been down with at all. But I wasn't going to break, and I think Mr. Jones was starting to figure that out. And I was pretty tired of this whole thing. The agents finished rifling through our stuff just as the power went out, which was the icing on the cake, let me tell you. I might not break, but that didn't mean I wouldn't flip out and totally lose it.

Mr. Jones sat for a minute, looking completely creepy in the shadowy living room, and then stood up and leaned over me. He was one tall guy, I have to give him that. "Trust me on this, Jeremy: If you're hiding anything from us, we'll find out. And you'll wish to God you'd told us everything."

"Great, good to know," I said, not quite keeping my voice steady. As long as Agatha and Jack stayed in

Mrs. Simmons' apartment, we were golden. I just kept repeating that to myself. The Suits would never find out. Besides, I didn't want to think what would happen if I confessed to lying now.

Mr. Jones stared at me, his face so close that I could smell cigarette smoke on his breath. I ignored him.

"Don't underestimate us." He picked up the cheap ballpoint pen he'd been using to take notes during the interrogation and held it in front of my face. "You have no idea what we can do."

He clicked the pen once. And the power came back on.

"You'll be seeing me again, son," Mr. Jones said, tapping me not so lightly on the shoulder.

I just nodded. I think if I'd tried to do anything else I would've disintegrated into a puddle of goo on the floor.

I managed to fold my arms and stay upright as Mr. Jones left the apartment. But as soon as the door clicked shut, I shot over to the window and leaned against the

ledge, panting like I'd just run a marathon or something. I was a mess. I didn't even want to think about
how Mr. Jones had managed that trick with the pen.
And I really didn't want to think about what he was going to
do to us when he found out we had Jack. Because I didn't
believe for a minute that Agatha's lamebrain plan might
actually work. They might not be FBI or CIA, but they
were something, and it was something bad. They'd find
out. I was practically hyperventilating when I saw Mr.
Jones and Mr. Suit #2 get into the long black car with the
other Suits and drive away. Just like Agatha had pre-
dicted they would.

I slumped against the wall for a quick, two-second
mental breakdown and then took the stairs two at a time
back down to Mrs. Simmons' apartment. I didn't even
knock, I just busted inside.

Just in time, it looked like. Agatha's hair was done
up in what I'd call a bird's nest style, and the Dora suitcase was thumping angrily across the floor. Mrs. Simmons
didn't seem to notice, though. She was too busy quizzing

Agatha about every tiny detail about Dog in a Box and Professor Twitchett.

"So he's a night owl, you say? How long do you walk him? Does he like kibble? Not a morning person, right?"

Agatha nodded wearily. I think the bird's nest symbolized her last line of defense against Mrs. Simmons. "Not a morning person," she repeated dully.

"Just like Mrs. Garcia. She makes cookies. Interesting. Does he wear a collar? What's his favorite breakfast food? Is he housebroken? Any secret hiding places? Aliases or secret identities?" Honestly, after a couple of seconds it was tough to figure out which questions were about who. And Mrs. Simmons' Twitchett fixation seemed a little unhealthy if you asked me. More than just your basic crush. She was more like a homebound stalker. Kind of sad.

Agatha jumped to her feet when she noticed me standing there and scooped up the Dora suitcase, her hair sticking straight out on the left side. "Thanks, Mrs.

Simmons, gotta go!" She shot out of the door so fast I think her hair scratched my cheek. It was pointy and sharp, that's what I'm saying. I don't even know what you have to do to hair to make it like that.

"Thanks, Mrs. S," I said, slamming the door after us. Mrs. Simmons actually looked sorry to see us go.

Agatha was slumped on the couch when I walked in, her head flopped back against the cushions so she was staring up at the ceiling. "Are they gone? Did it work?"

"They're gone. I hope it worked."

Agatha didn't move. "Please. I need a comb. Please."

I understood. My time with Mrs. Simmons had been traumatic enough, and we hadn't been playing Beauty Parlor.

I looked around for a comb and found a brush on the coffee table, which I figured was the same thing. I handed it to Agatha (or, really, tossed it onto her lap) just as the Dora suitcase leapt a foot into the air.

"I think we better let him out for a little bit. He's not happy."

"I'm not happy." Agatha still hadn't moved.

"Comb your hair, Agatha," I said. Seriously, those Suit guys should hire Mrs. Simmons to do their interrogations—five more minutes with her and Agatha would've been handing over her e-mail passwords, locker combination, you name it.

I unzipped the Dora suitcase and the jackalope jumped out, hissing and spitting at me. I stumbled back as he hunched in the middle of the room, baring his teeth, bristling his fur, and slowly turning in a circle. I took another step back, trying to figure out which vital organs I should try to protect. But once he'd finished making the circle, Jack just sat down and started licking himself.

Pretty scary stuff.

Personally, I was pretty much over the whole jackalope thing. Maybe it was the stress of the morning, but compared to Mr. Jones, that jackalope was a marshmallow. By now I was like, sharp antlers, scary teeth, killer instinct, blah, blah, blah. The thing had tufty paws and a button nose and was waggling its soft cottony tail at me. Oh, the nightmares. At this point, I figured even if he ripped my throat out, at least my killer would look cute on the wanted poster.

Besides, I think the little guy was starting to look up to me. Imprinting on me or whatever. It probably was inevitable, since he knew I was looking out for him.

I flopped down onto the couch next to Agatha and plunked my head back to stare at the ceiling too.

"So that's it? The problems are over?" Agatha said after a long silence. The only sounds were of jackalope grooming.

"Yeah," I said. Sure. If you didn't count the problem of the freaking mutant sitting in the middle of the floor, we were all clear.

"We should probably search Twitchett's apartment. While they're gone, I mean. They'll probably come back for him."

"Probably."

Neither of us moved.

Finally, Agatha picked her head up and tentatively touched her hair. "How bad is it?"

I examined her head. I didn't want to sugarcoat it. All she had to do was look in a mirror to know the truth.

"It's pretty bad."

Agatha stuck the brush in near the top of her head and it stuck there. She sighed and dropped her hands like they were lead weights. "What's the point?"

I couldn't help it. I cracked up. Then Agatha cracked up and then we were both flopping around like beached fish, snorting and gasping for pretty much no reason.

I sat back up and wiped my eyes. And that's when I noticed the jackalope was gone.

"Where'd he go?" I squeaked, jumping to my feet.

Agatha scanned the room. No jackalope. "Relax, he couldn't have gone anywhere. Right?"

But I couldn't help remembering how quiet Mr. Jones had been on the stairs the first time I saw him. I hadn't heard anything suspicious just now. But then I hadn't been listening. Anything could have happened to him.

I was just starting to get that weird tight panicky feeling in my chest when a strange high shrieking noise came from the back of the apartment.

"Oh, no," Agatha said, racing down the hall. "HORTENSE!"

I was behind her by like two seconds, but close enough that I saw the whole thing.

Hortense was shrieking and slamming against the side of her cage, trying to get to Jack, and Jack was slashing his antlers at the cage sides, trying to get at Hortense. It looked like it was going to be a real bloodbath. Because even without the antler advantage, Hortense is a real bruiser. Saliva was dripping from her long orange teeth. And that thin wire was the only thing keeping them from each other's throats. Which is why I was surprised when Agatha reached down and opened Hortense's cage.

Jack and Hortense threw themselves at each other and it was like the biggest mushiest airport reunion you've ever seen: hugging, kissing, happy jumping. It was better than them killing each other, I guess, but not as exciting. Definitely not something I'd watch on pay-per-view.

"See? She knows it's her kid," Agatha said, pointing at Hortense, who was carefully grooming the tuft of hair between the jackalope's antlers. "Take that, Twitchett. Proof of your thievery, you loser."

Which, for Agatha, was a pretty mild statement.

I watched the jackalope snuggling down and trying hard not to skewer his mom on his killer antlers. It was cute. But something was bugging me.

"Hey, Agatha."

"Yeah?" She had this goofy grin on her face.

"That voice earlier? Who was that? In the hall?"

Agatha frowned at me and shrugged. "Beats me."

"But there was nobody upstairs? I mean, Mr. Jones was in my apartment when I got up there. He wasn't out in the hall."

"Well, he must've been earlier, right? Who cares." Agatha had squinched her face up completely now, like she was seriously irritated. But I wasn't going to let it go.

I looked back at the jackalope. "You know, jacka-lopes are supposed to be able to imitate humans. And throw their voices."

Agatha scowled at me. "Really? Great. Except he's not a jackalope. He's an animal hybrid. Get a grip, Jeremy. Jackalopes aren't real."

"Yeah, well, I'm just saying . . ."

"Yeah, well, I'm just saying you're an idiot. Hor-tense is his mom, get it? And she's not a jackalope. He's just a bunny whose DNA has been manipulated so he'll have bony protrusions growing out of his head. That's all."

Well, when you put it that way. But it sounded more like a convenient excuse to me. "Yeah, but when you think about it—"

"You know? We'd better go search Twitchett's place now, if we're going to. They'll be back soon." Agatha reached up and dragged the hairbrush out of her hair. Which had to hurt—a big clump of hair came out with it. But she totally ignored it and started brushing furiously. She shot a look at the lovefest on the floor. "They'll be safe here."

"What if someone comes in? Mr. Suit or someone?"

"Then they'll kill him."

That was probably true, actually. I wouldn't want to try my chances against that pair, pen tricks or no pen tricks.

I followed Agatha upstairs, and let me tell you, it's a good thing the Suit guys had left. Because one, Agatha's hair would've scared the pants off them, and two, she wasn't even trying to be quiet. I thought her feet were going to go through the stairs, she was stomping so hard.

I couldn't stop thinking about Jack and his voice throwing, though. I mean, come on, we all knew that's what had happened. And having a pet with a skill like that? You could get away with pretty much anything. You'd be like a superhero or something, with a cool jackalope sidekick to hang out with. I was beginning to see why everybody wanted the little guy so much. It kind of sucked to just hand something that awesome over to a crackpot like Twitchett.

When we got to Twitchett's apartment, Agatha dug around in her hair and came out with a hairpin. She fiddled with the lock for just a second before it seemed to recognize her and give up completely. Then she practically kicked the door in and stomped inside. I think I ticked her off with the jackalope stuff. But at least it perked her up.

I peeked inside after her, because honestly, it probably would've been a better idea to make sure there wasn't anyone inside the apartment before we just busted in. Agatha's one lucky chick, because the apartment was empty. Cleared out. (Well, except for his furniture and stuff. Like anyone would take that.) It was just like the office—completely clean and organized, like a model home or something.

I took a step inside and then hesitated. Everything about that apartment felt wrong. It even smelled wrong. It was like we were at the apartment of Twitchett's evil twin. Not the kind of thing I like to mess with, personally.

Agatha had already checked out the bedroom by the time I'd decided to suck it up and go inside.

"Well, this is ridiculous," Agatha said, dragging her brush through her hair again. "The guest towel is folded. It's *folded*, Jeremy. What's going on here?"

I shrugged. I didn't even know Twitchett had a guest towel.

"His suitcases are still here, there are clothes hanging neatly in the closet, and his stuff is all lined up on his dresser. *Lined up*. And I haven't seen a single book or paper in the place." Agatha pulled out a dining room chair with her foot and threw herself into it. So much for searching the apartment.

"Yeah, okay. So where do you want to search first?" I looked around the apartment. Agatha was right. The sooner we could get out of here the better.

Agatha rolled her eyes. "Weren't you listening? There's no point, Jeremy! His papers are gone. His books are gone. His computer is gone. And don't even tell me he took them. It's *them*. It's the Suit guys. They've taken everything and tried to make it look normal."

I felt a prickling on the back of my neck. "The towel was folded?"

"Folded. And the bed was made. There was an embroidered pillow, Jeremy. One I've never seen before. Propped against the headboard. It said 'Confession Is Good for the Soul.'"

Okay, that was weird. Yeah, I tried to keep out of Twitchett's toxic waste dump of an apartment, and maybe he could've hired a housekeeper or a maid or a hazmat crew. But an embroidered pillow? With a confession motto? I wrinkled my nose and realized why the apartment smelled so wrong. It wasn't just that it smelled lemony and clean. It was the smell underneath that—a cigarette smell I'd probably be having nightmares about for the rest of my life. We had to get out of there.

"That's it then," I said. "We're done here."

Agatha sighed and heaved herself up. "It's over. There's nothing to find." She trudged out of the apartment and locked the door behind us. The gloom of the hallway was a relief after that weird evil cleanness. I could almost pretend it wasn't real.

Agatha hovered in the hallway, fiddling with the brush. "You can leave the hybrid with me, I guess. Hortense likes him."

I narrowed my eyes. "Nice try, Agatha, but no way. You can't use Jack in the science fair." Plus she'd been pretty lackadaisical when he disappeared from the living room. Jack needs someone who looks out for him.

Agatha smacked me with the brush. "No kidding, you think I want those guys to come back? There's no way he can be my project now. I was just thinking with your mom . . ."

She had a point. We weren't really a household that was set up for a jackalope. Even if I shaved him bald, my mom would probably still be allergic.

"Just until we find Twitchett," she said. "He'll come back soon."

Or until I come up with a plan, I thought. But I nodded. It's not like I had any choice. "Yeah, I guess. Okay. So . . . later."

"Yeah, later." We did a really awkward kind of wave thing, and then Agatha headed downstairs. It was really weird and anticlimactic.

I unlocked the door to my apartment and did a once-over of the place just to make sure there weren't any Mr. Suit types hiding under the bed. But I didn't find anything. (I say once-over, but it was actually four or five once-overs. I wanted to be sure.) But I was alone.

I sat down at the kitchen table and fiddled with a twist tie. I didn't know what to do with myself. Technically, I wasn't even supposed to be home, since it was a school day and all. And even though it felt like the day had been thirty years long, it wasn't even noon.

After I demolished the twist tie, three napkins, and a flyer about a car wash, I felt better. I headed into my room and lay down on the bed. I figured I'd earned a nap. And it's not like anyone was there to stop me.

I'd barely closed my eyes when the knocking started. It was frantic, more like pounding, actually. I don't know if people can levitate, but I swear I almost hit the ceiling in my rush to get to the door.

I flung the door open, sure that it was going to be Professor Twitchett standing on the mat. But it wasn't. It was Agatha.

She pushed past me into the room and slammed the door behind her. "I got a note," she hissed, looking around nervously.

"Where?" She didn't have to tell me who it was from. There was only one person who would be leaving us notes.

"I was trying to feed the hybrid, but he didn't want a carrot for some reason. And there was a knock on the door. I opened it, but there was no one there. That's when I saw the note in the gargoyle mouth."

Twitchett. I nodded. "What did he say?"

Agatha opened her sweaty fist and I took the note that was clenched inside.

Zoo. 3:00. Bring my experiment.

I stared at the note, trying to get my brain to work. "What do you think?"

"It's pretty sloppy, but I guess it's his handwriting. But it's not really his style, is it? And he doesn't say anything about the hybrid."

"But he wouldn't want to be specific in case someone else found it." I stared at the note again. I wished Agatha hadn't sweated all over the ink. It's hard to judge hand-writing when it's all smeary. "It was in the right place."

"True." Agatha bit her lip. "We should go."

"But—" I hesitated. "Why did he knock on your door? Why not mine? He told me not to tell you." Sorry to be rude, but he did.

"I know. Maybe Bob told him I came by?" Agatha took the note back and put it in her pocket. "We should go, just in case. We'll be smart and keep our eyes open. I'll get the hybrid."

I didn't like it, but I didn't know what else we could do. "So we'll meet a little before three and head over."

Agatha nodded. She was just turning around to go downstairs when my phone rang. We both froze. It's amazing how scary a ringing phone can be when you're already on level ten freakout. We just stared at each other as it rang a second and third time, and then slowly I went over to it. It's my house, so I figured it had to be me. But I really didn't want to know who was on the other end.

I took a deep breath and answered it.

The connection was really crappy, and I couldn't even hear at first. Then all I could hear was breathing. I took a chance. "Professor Twitchett?"

"Jeremy, you have to go."

I nodded to Agatha and mouthed the word "Twitchett." "Don't worry, we are. We got your note. Zoo at three o'clock." I tried to ignore the fact that he'd called me Jeremy instead of Igor. He'd never done that before. "Right? Zoo at three? I'll meet you there?"

"*Jeremy*," Twitchett's voice sounded ragged and painful. "You have to go, *now*. GET OUT. Informant. They're in the building. *You're being watched.*"

10.

Agatha and I Entertain Tourists

You know those horror movies where people move into a fancy old house and then the house goes "GET OUT" and the people go, "My, what a strange sound! I'll just unpack the china now." And they don't get out?

We got out.

I don't even know if I hung up the phone, that's how fast we were moving. Agatha was downstairs with that suitcase zipped before Jack even realized he was back inside. Our feet were like the Road Runner's feet when he really gets going, just spinny wheels. I was going so fast I almost hadn't caught the last few words Twitchett whispered into the phone. The ones I hadn't told Agatha about yet.

Theoretically, getting out was the right thing to do. We definitely couldn't stay there, not if we were being watched. But once we were out on the street dragging the jackalope behind us in the Dora the Explorer suitcase, we were stuck. We didn't have any place to go.

"Well, home's out, school's out. The lab? Maybe Bob could help?" Agatha looked up hopefully.

"Yeah, right. The hair tousler? I don't think so." I couldn't put my finger on it, but something about that guy still bugged me. Besides, I think if Twitchett had intended us to go to Bob, he would've said something along the lines of "Go to Bob." And that's not what he said.

"Well, wandering around isn't doing us any good. We need to make a plan." Agatha plunked down abruptly on the curb and started rooting around in her book bag. I sat down next to her. She was right. It felt like we'd been walking forever, and I didn't want to be the kind of guy who wanders the streets with a pink cartoon character suitcase. (I know, too late, right?)

Agatha pulled out a spiral notebook and started tapping her pencil thoughtfully against her teeth. "We need someplace to go where nobody's going to bug us. Someplace where we won't stand out."

"And someplace where a jackalope can get a little breathing space," I said, watching the fabric on the Dora suitcase ripple. You could see the prongs of the jackalope's antlers almost poking through in the corners. Just call him Quality Inspector Number Four.

Agatha stopped tapping for a second and frowned. "Right. Breathing space."

I hoped she was better at coming up with ideas than I was, because I was totally drawing a blank. Even someplace like the mall would be too risky for us, what with the high-tech teenage sensors they seem to have down there. Those guards are always giving me grief, and that's when I'm just hanging out, not carrying a top-secret imaginary killer in my wussy suitcase.

Agatha started tapping again. Apparently tapping is a big part of her brainstorming process. I watched a white van turn onto our street up the block. That tapping was starting to get on my nerves.

"Any ideas?"

Agatha stopped tapping and suddenly grinned an evil grin. "Oh yeah. I know just the thing."

I was impressed. "Cool, so what do you think?"

"Okay, this is what we do. We—" Agatha stood up abruptly and grabbed me by the arm. "Get the suitcase and come on."

She started walking briskly down the street, looking straight ahead. I scrambled to my feet and hurried after her.

"What? What's the deal? We what?"

"We get out of here, that's what. That white van has driven by three times." Agatha didn't even turn her head, but of course I whipped my head around like an idiot just in time to see the white van driving off down the block. Slowly.

Since I was already rubbernecking, I tried to get a look inside, but windows were tinted or something. Which is never a good sign.

"Why is it always a white van?" Agatha said through gritted teeth. "Don't criminals have any imagination?"

"What do you mean?"

"It's always a stupid white van! Every time! Read the newspaper sometime, Einstein."

The white van turned the corner up ahead. Agatha whipped around. "Quick, before they come back. We've got to split up. Give me the hybrid."

I pulled the suitcase closer to myself. "No way."

"We don't have time to argue about this! Give me the hybrid and we meet up in one hour." Agatha snatched at the suitcase again.

I shook my head. Don't ask me why I was so eager to be saddled with a hot pink girly suitcase for an hour, but I was. She wasn't getting Jack. She couldn't keep him safe like I could.

"Forget it. The jackalope stays with me."

Agatha swore in frustration and shot a look over my shoulder. The street was still clear, but not for long. "Fine! Fine, whatever. Meet me in one hour. The fountain in the middle of town. Across from the Grand Empyrean Hotel."

I nodded, but apparently I was taking too long, because Agatha pushed me in the chest so hard I stumbled off the curb. "Now GO!" she said. She turned and took off running in the opposite direction, her long hair streaming out behind her.

I picked myself up, grabbed the suitcase, ran across the street, and ducked behind a 7-Eleven just in time to see the white van drive by again. I crouched behind the Dumpster until it had gone by once and then a second time. I waited, but it didn't come by a third time.

I hoped Agatha had gotten away too. I checked my watch. I wasn't sure what to do with myself. I didn't want to start wandering again, not with whoever was in that van looking for me. But I didn't feel like spending the next hour crouching behind a Dumpster, either. Besides, my knees were killing me.

There was a grassy patch behind the store, so I headed over to it and sat down. The jackalope hadn't been very twitchy lately, so I unzipped the suitcase a bit to peek inside.

Two glowing eyes glared back at me, which I guess meant he was fine. (Ticked off, but fine.) I zipped him back up and did some of Coach Reynolds' deep breathing to clear my head. I would've felt better if I had some idea what Agatha's plan was. Meeting at the fountain in an hour didn't give me a heck of a lot to go on.

I picked up a crumbly-looking stick on the ground and started shredding it. Agatha seemed to have big ideas, but Agatha hadn't been on the phone with Twitchett. Agatha hadn't heard those last few words he'd said. And I didn't know why I hadn't told her.

Except, deep down, I did know.

I bit my lip and threw the stick away. Twitchett had said there was an informant. Someone in the building, that was one of the last things he said. And I couldn't help but remember that one of the first things he'd told me, in that note when this whole thing started, was not to tell Agatha.

It made a lot of sense. Twitchett and Agatha had had a falling-out. She said it was about him stealing her ideas, but I didn't really know that, did I? And if Twitchett was warning me about someone in the building, who else could it really be? My mom? The flight attendant who was never home? The crazy shut-in lady or the cookie couple? He didn't know any of them like he knew Agatha.

And I couldn't help but remember that the entire time I'd been grilled by Mr. Jones (Agatha's idea), she'd been on her own. Supposedly in Mrs. Simmons' apartment, but again, I didn't know that for sure. And then the Suits had left, just like Agatha had told me they would. Almost like she'd planned it.

The whole thing made me feel cold in the pit of my stomach. I didn't want to believe it, but it's not like I knew what to believe. There wasn't a single person I knew I could trust.

There was one thing I knew, though. I sure as hell wasn't meeting Agatha at the fountain.

Yeah, I know I was probably being stupid, but I had to trust my gut. And my gut was telling me to take care of number one. Me. (And I guess also number two: Jack.) Besides, if she wasn't the informant, she'd be better off out of the whole thing.

I got up, dusted my butt off and headed into town with my wussy pink suitcase. I wasn't going to skulk in the bushes for the rest of my life. I was going to take action.

So what if I didn't know what that action was yet? That wasn't the point.

I'd told Agatha that Twitchett had told us to get out. And that was true. But I hadn't told her those last two words he'd said. And that was a huge relief. Because without those last two words, she didn't have the whole picture. And I wouldn't need to worry about her showing up when I met Twitchett later on. Or spilling the beans to the Feds.

The last thing he'd said, after he'd told me to get out, was just for me. Two words that sound pretty lame unless you know what they mean. So brace yourself for lameness. Those two words he said? "Señor Slappy."

(Okay, shut up and stop laughing.) I know, dumb, huh? It wouldn't mean a thing to those Mr. Suit types, and it wouldn't mean a thing to Agatha. But I knew exactly what he meant. So I knew where to meet him.

The sea lion pool at the zoo.

There's this big old sea lion at the zoo who lives to splash people. He lures people close, being all friendly and inviting, and then when they get near enough, he slaps the water with his giant flipper and they get a huge faceful of water. Then he laughs his butt off. Privately, I've always thought of him as Señor Slappy, and I'd let the nickname slip to Twitchett a week or two ago when I'd accidentally sprayed myself in the face at the sink. He didn't seem to care, so I'm surprised he even remembered.

But when he whispered "Señor Slappy," I knew just what he meant.

I still wasn't sure about that note that Agatha got (or claimed to have gotten. For all I knew, she wrote the stupid thing herself. Pretty convenient that it was too smudgy to ID the handwriting). But I figured three was as good a time as any to head over to the Señor. So I still had a couple of hours to kick around before me and Jack went to feed the seals.

I'd wandered downtown and was pretty much doing my aimless wandering thing when I realized I was only about three blocks from the Grand Empyrean. I glanced at my watch. Only a few minutes before I was supposed to meet Agatha. I turned around to go in the opposite direction, and then I hesitated.

If I got there early, I might see her talking to the Suit goons. And if I saw the traitor meeting her goons in person, I'd know for sure I couldn't trust her, plus I could rub her face in it later. So I turned back around and hustled over to the plaza with the fountain. I'm not an idiot, though—I didn't go wait in front of the fountain like a doofus. Instead I pulled out my sunglasses, bought a baseball cap from the drugstore on the corner, and positioned myself behind a postcard rack down the street from the fountain. (My masterstroke? I bought a Yankees cap. Everybody knows how much I hate the Yankees. Genius, if I do say so myself.)

I couldn't help but grin. She'd never spot me.

I watched the people at the fountain, but frankly, they were pretty boring. There was a mom with the most elaborate stroller I'd ever seen, probably fully equipped with GPS and a helipad. Her kid wasn't in it, though; he was too busy touching the water in the fountain and then shrieking and running in circles. There was a business guy in a suit (but not a *Suit* suit) talking on one of those ear cell phone hookups, a French girl with a beret and chin-length black hair, and a couple of tourists taking pictures of each other. Another chick was just standing around looking awfully suspicious, but after a few minutes she put on an apron for the coffee shop next door and went back to work. So probably just a barista.

I watched until my eyeballs got too bored and then I looked at the exciting postcard display again. But there are only so many times you can look at a picture of a Civil War guy on a horse saying "Wish you were here" before your brain starts to dribble out of your ears.

I checked my watch. It was five minutes past when Agatha was supposed to show. But there was no sign of her.

I tried to turn the postcard rack for a little variety, but it must've been rusted solid, because it just screamed in protest and refused to move. I checked the fountain again. Still no Agatha. And no real change, except that the French girl was gone, and the tourists were arguing over a map.

I didn't want to blow my cover, but there didn't seem to be anyone around. So I decided it was safe to abandon the postcard area. I'd only taken a couple of steps when I slammed right into the French girl.

Who promptly cussed me out in a completely non French accent.

"I knew you were going to pull something! I knew I couldn't trust you!" she hissed, her beret sliding down over one eye. "You're the informant! I knew it!"

I blinked. There was no mistaking that talent for swearing.

"Agatha?" I peered down into the face. It was definitely her.

"Who do you think, dipstick? What were you doing skulking over here? I spotted you a mile away." Agatha pushed the beret back up and glared at me.

"Excuse me if my disguise isn't elaborate enough for you. I didn't know the plan involved a skanky wig,"

I said. I was definitely offended. Didn't she notice the Yankees cap? So I didn't buy a French-looking black wig and a beret, big deal. Who would fall for that anyway?

"A wig? A wig wouldn't keep you from looking like the most average boring guy on the planet. But most guys don't go around town with a hot pink suitcase, brainiac."

I glanced down at the jackalope and said a couple of choice swearwords of my own. Yeah, probably should've thought to camouflage that. Dora was pretty distinctive.

"So what? At least I'm not a filthy spy," I shot back. "You're the one who's the informant."

"Have you gone mental?" Agatha spat. "If I were the informant, why would I have shown you the note?"

"How do I even know that was from Twitchett?" I said angrily. "Maybe you're setting me up!"

"*I had the hybrid!*" Agatha said, a little too loudly. "I could have just *left*."

Which was a valid point, and one I hadn't thought of. Kind of made the whole suspecting Agatha thing feel kind of stupid. I glanced around. We were attracting attention, which, for people on the run, is not a good idea. The tourists had stopped arguing over the map and were taking pictures of us. Not good.

I pulled Agatha behind the postcard rack and blocked our faces with a yellowing postcard of a kitten hanging from a branch saying "Hang in there!" It had to be seventy years old at least. "Look, I'm not an informant, okay?"

"Well, I'm not either. I can't *believe* you. Thanks a lot." Agatha wiped her nose.

She shook a shopping bag at me. "After I got supplies and everything!"

I looked at the bag. "Supplies?"

Agatha smirked at me. "Disposable cell phones, that kind of thing. I figured we could use them if we have to split up again. Look, are we good? Because we shouldn't talk about this here." She looked around nervously, like she'd just realized we'd been screaming on the street. I didn't tell her about the tourists.

"We're good. So what now?" It wasn't a good idea, but I didn't think I could shake her without a scene. I'd keep an eye on her. If it turned out later that she was a filthy spy, I'd sic Jack on her. Besides, if she wasn't a filthy spy, and she really thought I was, I didn't want to make her suspicious. I cussed Professor Twitchett out in my head. This thing had gotten so twisted around, I wasn't sure I even trusted myself anymore. Way to be specific about the informant, Twitchett.

Agatha adjusted her beret. "Now we hide."

Call me lame, but hiding sounded awesome. "Great. Where?" I looked around the plaza. Not a lot of great hiding places were jumping out at me.

Agatha hitched her shopping bag back over her shoulder. "Where else? The Grand Empyrean."

11.

I Meet My New Dad

This might be a good time to apologize to the house-keeping staff of the Grand Empyrean. They seem like good people, and they really didn't deserve all the trouble we brought to their hotel. As far as I know, they don't usually have mythical creatures running around trashing the rooms.

The Grand Empyrean is one of the biggest hotels in town—one of those really fancy ones with all the gold trim inside. The kind where the guys in tuxedos stand outside and open doors for the guests. Not your roadside motel, is what I'm saying. Not a place that I ever would've tried to sneak in, because those tuxedo guys, they're real bruisers. They'll kick you to the curb.

So you know I was super thrilled that Agatha was heading straight for the front doors. Because unless I was suddenly striking out on my own, I was going in too. I tried to look like I belonged. At least I had a suitcase, right?

Agatha marched straight up the steps and stopped, waiting for the tuxedo guy to open the door for her. Which he did. It was pretty shocking, actually. He didn't even make a face or any snarky comments about my suitcase. (Which, come on, how could he resist?)

We breezed on in like we had every right to be there, and unfortunately, that's where I lost it a little bit. I'll admit it. I stopped to gawk. I've never seen anything as fancy as that lobby.

"Keep walking," Agatha hissed, smiling at the man at the concierge desk.

I kept walking, but man, it wasn't easy. There were fountains and fireplaces and chandeliers and carpets so thick I swear I was three inches shorter than usual. Which, to be honest, didn't really do a lot for my self-esteem. I definitely breathed a sigh of relief when we got past the carpeted check-in area. I was almost feeling normal again when we went through an archway and ended up in the middle of what looked for all the world like a high-end mall.

"There are stores in here," I said, trying to pretend the lady behind the jewelry counter across from me wasn't staring. "What kind of hotel has a mall?"

"Shut up and help me find the Business Center," Agatha said out of the corner of her mouth. She smiled at the jewelry woman, who suddenly got very busy rearranging the countertop.

Lucky for me, I can read, so finding the Business Center wasn't that difficult. The gigantic sign on the wall up ahead that said "Business Center" was a big tip-off.

I pointed it out to Agatha (who didn't even say thank you) and followed as she hurried in and sat down at a computer. Luckily none of the people hanging out at the luxury hotel had any business needs at the moment. Probably all shopping at the hotel mall.

"What are you doing?" I said to Agatha, as she went online and called up the Grand Empyrean website.

"Just learn from the master," Agatha said. She clicked a couple of times, blocking my view of the screen with her big head, and then turned around. "Standard okay, or do you think we should get a deluxe?"

"What?"

"Standard is probably fine. We won't be here long," Agatha said and went back to clicking and blocking.

Then she clicked one final time and spun around in the desk chair with a grin. "Phase one complete."

"Phase one of what?"

"The plan. We've got reservations. Phase two: Check in."

"What, here? Are you insane?" I tried to keep my voice calm. "They're never going to let a couple of kids check in; you know that, Agatha. Even *with* the Dora suitcase." Somebody had to be the voice of reason. Agatha had really lost it.

Agatha rolled her eyes. "Of course they won't. That's why they're not going to see us."

She picked up her shopping bag and headed back through the archway to the check-in area. Then she bent down and pretended to tie her shoe. "That is where I'm going."

She jerked her head at a sleek ATM-type machine in the corner of the lobby, near a bunch of trees decorated with twinkly lights. (Yeah, I know. Trees inside. It was that kind of place.) "You are going to the counter to make a disturbance of some kind. I don't care what it is, as long as you're obnoxious or stupid enough to attract everyone's attention. Shouldn't be hard for you."

"Agatha, they're not going to give us a room. We're going to get busted." I was starting to feel panicky.

Agatha ignored me. "When you're done, meet me back at the Business Center. Just keep them distracted. And don't get yourself thrown out."

I was liking this plan less and less. "But wait, what?"

"Oh, sheesh, Jeremy, just be yourself." Agatha gave me a shove in the direction of the desk and started off toward the weird, unnatural indoor trees.

She was halfway across the room before I actually believed she was serious. But there was no way to stop her, and even though the concierge was just lazily flipping his pen around on his desk, I could tell he already had her in his sights. It didn't look like I had much choice, unless I wanted to watch Agatha get interrogated.

I headed to the check-in desk to create a diversion, which seemed like the world's worst plan ever.

I looked around carefully to make sure that there was no one around who might know me from school or identify me in a future life. Because not wanting to get kicked out was severely limiting my diversion options here. And the only option I could think of was going to ruin my reputation at school if anyone found out (even more than being at an actual hotel with Agatha Hotchkins).

I tried to make my face look as babyish as possible, sniffled loudly, and made my lip quiver as I went up to the counter. That's right: I was going to cry.

The sniffle caught the attention of the middle-aged woman standing nearest to me at the counter. She looked up suspiciously, probably trying to decide whether I was making a pathetic I'm-about-to-cry sniffle or a disgusting I'm-about-to-dribble-snot-on-your-counter sniffle. That's why the lip quiver was key. When she noticed that, she was putty in my hands.

"Can you tell me if my dad's checked in yet? He's supposed to be here, but he's not answering his cell phone. I've called and called." I sniffled again and tried to look brave. I dug my feet down in the thick carpet until I'd sunk down to the height of your average fourth grader and tried not to watch Agatha sidling up to the fancy machine.

The lady looked sympathetic. "Let me just look that up for you. What's the name?"

I sniffled louder. "Well, see that's the thing. He's kind of well-known? So he doesn't use his real name when he's traveling. So he probably just went with John Smith?"

I tried to peer over the desk at her computer while she tapped away. Then she frowned at me. "No, I'm sorry, we don't have a reservation for a John Smith."

I did a loud hiccup-sob that made the man next to her at the counter take notice, but only for a second. The concierge had stopped playing with his pen and was watching Agatha intently. I was going to have to ramp up my game if this was going to work as a diversion. A couple of sniffles apparently weren't going to cut it.

The concierge scooted his chair back. I took a deep breath. *Game on, concierge.*

"Are you sure?" I wailed, and then looked around like I was embarrassed. "What about John Brown—is there anyone under that name? Please?"

Even the concierge looked over when I did that last one. I felt a surge of triumph, which I channeled into another hiccupy sob. I almost had him. I hoped I was buying Agatha enough time.

"No, no John Brown. I'm sorry." The woman really did look sorry. The man down the counter didn't, though. He looked disgusted. Well, excuse me for living, buddy.

I snuffled loudly into my sleeve and tried to look panicky. Which wasn't hard, since the concierge was getting up. We were two seconds away from busted or home free. I just didn't know which.

"Those are the only names I know that he uses! Unless . . . Charles Smith? How about that one? I think he goes by that sometimes." I didn't see how I could act more panicked without wetting myself, and I'm sorry, there are just some things I'm not willing to do.

The woman started typing again, and the concierge came over and tapped me lightly on the shoulder. "Son, is everything okay?"

"Yeah," I snuffled sadly, trying to keep from laughing hysterically. I should be on TV, I'm that good. I clutched at the concierge's arm. "I don't know. I'm just trying to find my dad, but he won't answer his phone."

The desk woman tapped some more on the computer. "Charles Smith?"

"Yeah," I said, gearing up to produce a heartbreaking wail.

"Good news! He has checked in just a little while ago."

Well, crap. Who would've thought I'd get it in three? In retrospect, I should've gone with more uncommon names, but I didn't want to be too obvious about it.

"That's . . . uh . . . great. Thanks." I didn't know what to do except stand there like an idiot.

"Why don't I call up and let him know you're here?" The woman smiled at me again. The concierge patted me on the shoulder and headed back over to his desk.

Why don't you just shoot me now, lady?

"No, that's okay, you don't have to—"

"No trouble at all!" The woman said, ear already to the phone. "Mr. Smith? Your son is in the lobby."

I swear my heart stopped beating. Once Charles Smith told her that he didn't have a son, it would only be a matter of seconds before guards had me in handcuffs and carted me off to jail.

I tightened my grip on the Dora suitcase and got ready to bolt. But just as I was flexing my knees for takeoff, the woman nodded encouragingly at me. "Thank you, sir. I'll let him know."

She hung up the phone. "Your father will be right down for you."

"Oh. Uh. Thanks, that's awesome," I said. I could feel sweat beading up on my head. "I really appreciate it. I'll just, uh, wait at the shops."

I turned around and walked awkwardly over to the mall area, with the desk woman beaming at me the whole way. I turned around and gave her a lame half wave, turned the corner, and took off as fast as I could toward the Business Center.

Agatha was already there waiting for me. "Not much of a diversion, Jeremy," she said. "But it was enough. Sorry about your dad." She smirked at me.

"It had better be! I almost got thrown in jail! I've got to get out of here because my 'father' is coming down for me!" Sheesh, one morning with Agatha and I was doing air quotes too.

"No problem," Agatha said. She waved a room key at me. "We'll just head upstairs."

"What the—"

Agatha went over and pushed the elevator button while I gawked at the key. "Where did you get that? Is that real?"

Agatha glared at me. "Shut it!"

The elevator door opened and a rumpled-looking businessman got out. He looked up and down the hallway with a confused look on his face. I had a really bad feeling I was up close and personal with one Mr. Charles Smith.

I pushed past him into the elevator and hit that close door button for all I was worth. I didn't stop until the doors were shut tight. Agatha smirked at me the whole way up.

We got out on the twelfth floor and walked the maze of passageways until we came to room 1231. Then Agatha opened the door with a flourish of the plastic card key, waltzed into the room, and started making herself at home right off. I was still waiting for the catch. I looked around. It was a real-life hotel room all right—a really fancy one, too. And no security guards seemed to be on our tail.

"Okay, what gives?" I folded my arms and waited for an explanation. "Are you a thief?"

"It's called online reservations, dumbbutt," Agatha said, throwing her shopping bag onto the bed.

"So where'd the key come in? Is this somebody's room?" Unless she'd crept around behind the counter while I was doing my "Where's dad?" act, I didn't see how she'd pulled it off.

"Yeah, mine. It's automatic check-in. You just go to the machine, use the credit card you used to make the reservation, and voilà! Instant room key." She flopped down into the big red chair by the TV and grinned like a maniac.

"Credit card?"

Agatha shrugged and propped her feet on the footstool. "My dad gave it to me. It's for emergencies. I figure this is an emergency, right?"

"They let you use a credit card?"

"It has my name on it and everything, okay? It's totally legit. I use it all the time."

"But won't your dad get mad?"

Agatha rolled her eyes. "Look, if he freaks, I'll just say the card was stolen. Why would I be reserving a room at the Grand Empyrean? In the middle of a school day? That's just ridiculous. Use your brain, Jeremy."

I have to admit I was impressed. Freaked out by her criminal mind, but impressed. Once my heart rate had gone back down to normal levels, I carefully unzipped the Dora suitcase and stood back to watch the traditional jackalope hissing and/or spitting show.

Then I hit the minibar.

"Bourbon counts as whiskey, right?" I said, looking at a couple of bottles. I opened one, put my finger over the top, and turned it over. I touched my finger to my tongue and then seriously wished I hadn't. The whiskey burned like all get-out and tasted like armpit. I don't know how Jack drinks that stuff.

"Great, I'm on the run with a drunk. Just my luck." Agatha hauled herself out of the big red chair and started rummaging in the shopping bag.

"Not for me, you jerk. For him. It's whiskey bourbon, right?" I was pocketing everything I could identify as whiskey. I didn't know how long we'd have him, and it's not like I could just go into a liquor store and explain that I had a jackalope to feed.

Agatha ripped the packaging off one of the disposable cell phones and tossed it to me. (Threw it at me, actually. It left a mark.) "What, does he care about brands too? He's not hungry. I tried to give him a carrot and he didn't want it. And even if he was hungry, he wouldn't want alcohol."

"Carrot? No wonder. Jackalopes like booze." I grabbed one of the glasses from the top of the minibar and took the protective cover off.

"But he's—" Agatha started, but I held up a hand and amazingly, it shut her up.

"An animal hybrid. I know. But he's not." I poured the bourbon into a glass and set it down next to Jack, who only sniffed it for a second before practically upending the glass in an attempt to guzzle it.

I grinned. "He's a jackalope."

12.

Presenting Señor Slappy

Can I just mention how much fun it is to spend an afternoon arguing the jackalope/animal hybrid question with Agatha? Because that's all we did. And I don't care how many times you tell me there are no such things as jackalopes, or how many different scientific theories and formulas you throw at me. If it looks like a jackalope and quacks like a jackalope, it's a jackalope.

The fact that the jackalope was lying on its back on the floor singing campfire songs wasn't helping her argument either.

"How did you teach him 'Happy Trails'?" Agatha asked after the argument had finally petered out.

"I didn't," I said, chucking the empty bourbon bottle into the trash. "Campfire songs are in his blood. You can look. It's on Wikipedia."

"Hmm," Agatha said, watching the jackalope wave a lazy paw in the air. "Hmm."

I checked my watch. "We should get going if we're going to meet Twitchett. I'll get him back in his suitcase."

"Maybe we should just leave him here." Agatha put her wig and beret back on.

Not to be a Negative Nancy, but that sounded like the world's worst idea. "We can't leave him here. Isn't the whole point to return him to Twitchett?"

Agatha just humphed at me and readjusted her beret.

"Agatha, he's a cute little guy, but we can't keep him hidden forever. And leaving him alone seems like a bad idea." I've heard about maids at hotels, always wanting to come in and tidy up. I wasn't going to have their blood on my hands.

Agatha shrugged. "Yeah, okay. But we're not handing him over unless it's really Twitchett."

"Trust me, it'll be him. He distinctly said the words 'Señor Slappy.'" And that's not the kind of thing that slips out by accident.

I'd considered trying to lose Agatha somewhere before the meet-up at the zoo until I realized that even if I did, she knew both the time (three o'clock) and the place (zoo). Even if she didn't know the specifics, it's not a big zoo; she'd figure it out. Besides, if I didn't trust someone, I'd totally lose it. So I went ahead and told Agatha the whole story about Señor Slappy and what Twitchett had said on the phone. Once she got done rolling around on the floor laughing like an idiot, she agreed that that was probably where we should look for him.

It was definitely easier packing a happy, singing jackalope than a crabby, anxious one. All I really had to do was flop Jack into the Dora suitcase and step aside while he let loose with a megaburp. I hesitated before zipping him up. It was probably the last time I was going to see the little guy. My last look at a mythical creature. I swallowed hard and zipped the zipper. The last thing

I needed was to get sentimental. Especially over a tiny killer I couldn't keep anyway.

Agatha eyed the suitcase critically. "I should've gotten you another backpack," she said. "That thing is way too distinctive."

"Yeah, too late now," I said. "Besides, in just a little while, it won't even matter anymore."

"I guess," Agatha said. But she still was giving the Dora suitcase dirty looks. I don't know why. I was the one toting it around looking like a loser.

We headed out, just like we were regular hotel patrons, which I guess we were, but wow, it felt weird.

The woman at the front desk gave me a confused wave as I went past, and the tuxedo guys even held the door for us. I could get used to this.

It was only about a ten-minute walk to the zoo, so before we knew it we were sitting on a bench, watching Señor Slappy target his next victims.

The sea lion pool is in the middle of the zoo, and it's one of the prime attractions. Most of the sea lions were doing laps underwater, only surfacing to blow snotty water around. But Señor Slappy was hovering near the edge of the tank, doing his best to smile at a woman with two little daughters. They didn't suspect a thing.

Señor Slappy was going all out, rolling on his back and waving his flippers, doing his best to be the cutest darn sea lion on the planet. And it was working. The mom with the daughters was laughing and getting closer and closer to the railing—the railing that was right up at the edge of the water. This was going to be good.

"Any time now," Agatha said, scanning the area. She didn't seem to be paying attention to Señor Slappy. I looked around too. For a second I'd forgotten what we were there for.

I just wished Twitchett would show so we could get this over with. I was going to be sorry to say goodbye to Jack, but sorry in a "Yeah, see ya" kind of way and not in a "We'll write every day" kind of way. The last thing I needed was some stinking jackalope hanging around all the time, even if he could help me skip out on curfew for the rest of my life. But still, I had a twinge or two. I'm not made of stone. I tried to make myself feel better by thinking about Twitchett's reward.

"There he is!" Agatha jumped to her feet and pointed to the other side of the sea lion pool. (More proof that Agatha's spy skills could use some improving.)

I peered across the pool. She was right. It was definitely Professor Twitchett.

Talk about working on your spy skills. For someone all into the whole cloak-and-dagger scene, Twitchett's were pretty bad. He wasn't in disguise at all—he was wearing one of his ratty cardigan sweaters and looking more rumpled than ever. And he was flat out barreling toward the sea lion pool. It was pretty obvious he was looking for me, but he wasn't the least bit worried about drawing attention to himself. He almost slammed into a couple strolling by, and when he saw me, he yelled my name and waved. Way to be low-key, Twitchett.

And after the day we'd had, I was really not down with him being so obvious. It made me pretty jumpy. And I only got jumpier when the screaming started.

I should've seen it coming—after all, I'd seen Señor Slappy's windup routine. I should've been waiting for the pitch. But when he caught those two kids with a faceful of fishy water, the shrieking really threw me.

Twitchett didn't even turn a hair; he just pushed past the two dripping, screaming kids and their poor mother and hurried over to me.

He pointed at Agatha, a look of horror on his face. "Jeremy, what's she doing here? I told you not to involve Agatha!" Like she wasn't standing right there and couldn't hear him.

"Because she's the informant?" I had to know. I don't even think Agatha heard me, she was getting so ragey.

"Yeah, wonder why, you thieving *rat fink*!" Agatha got right up in Twitchett's face.

"Now, that's hardly fair. Your ideas were undeveloped and rudimentary. I may have been developing a parallel theory . . ."

"It was my idea, and you flat-out stole it! Just like you steal *everything*." Agatha's spit glands must've been working overtime, because she sprayed everybody within a four-foot radius. She was almost as good as Señor Slappy.

Standing around watching people fight isn't my idea of a good time. I was definitely rethinking this whole meeting plan. I glanced around nervously. This place was way too exposed for us to get into a brawl. Somebody needed to be the grown-up here.

I pushed in between them. "Okay, I got it, you hate each other. Now shut it. We've got big problems here. Twitchett, what's up with the guys in suits? They've been chasing us all day."

Professor Twitchett turned a shade paler. "They have? Men in suits? They're here?"

Talk about not making any sense. Twitchett was up for the prize.

I stared at him like he'd sprouted horns and a third eye. "Come on, Twitchett, you know that! You warned us about them! Didn't you?"

Professor Twitchett ran his hand through his hair and looked around.

I waved a hand in front of his face. Pretty rude, I know, but I was frustrated. "Hello? On the phone? Remember? You said, 'informant, get out?' What was all that if it wasn't about the Suits?" I was starting to think Agatha had the right idea. I wanted to grab Twitchett by the ratty sweater and do some serious shaking.

Twitchett gave a nervous cough. "Did they get my . . . my project?"

"The jackalope?"

"Animal hybrid." Agatha glared at me.

I glared back. "They didn't get it. It's still safe." I patted the Dora suitcase. "But who are those guys, Professor Twitchett?"

Professor Twitchett looked uncomfortable. "If the men following you are the men I think they are, they work for . . . well, I . . . I seem to have run afoul of the government, Jeremy."

Well, no duh. Thanks for the news flash. "Yeah, we figured," I said. "Who are they? What did you do?"

"You saw my project. I was very proud of my work.

I explained this all, Jeremy. In the note with the . . . item in question. I may have been a bit . . . unwise in my confidences."

"That note got eaten," I said.

"Just cut to the chase, Twitchett," Agatha spat. I was glad she was getting as sick of his dancing around as I was. "What did you do?"

"Bragging. I did a little bragging. I got in a bit over my head." Professor Twitchett blushed. "The gentlemen you met came to me with a proposal that I found unacceptable. Apparently it wasn't up for negotiation. But I didn't expect them so soon . . ."

"How did they even find out? Who did you tell?" I shot a nasty look at Agatha. Not that I thought she was a big mouth, but . . .

"I may have said a few things . . . online." Twitchett cringed. "Anonymously, of course."

"You did *not*!" Agatha said. "Are you a *total idiot*?"

Well yeah, I'd say so. But I thought it might be mean, so I didn't.

"I realize now those forums were less than private, Agatha." Twitchett glared at her. "But I didn't know that at the time. I thought I was among colleagues. I didn't realize they were under surveillance by DARPA."

Seriously, I didn't even know what that meant. I must've been absent the day we had our Understanding Crazy People tutorial. I tried to tell Twitchett to try speaking English, but he cut me off. "I was foolish. Very foolish. Understood. I never meant to involve you with the government, I was simply trying to hide the project from . . ." He shook his head. "Now, please, give me my project. I need to complete my research." He pulled a canvas sack out of his satchel. "Please. Give me the Subject."

A canvas sack? That didn't sit well with me for some reason. And it sure wasn't going to sit well with Jack. I just stared at it. And suddenly Twitchett didn't seem any better than Mr. Jones. "I, uh . . ."

"You say you didn't know the men were after us. Right? Those guys in suits? Total surprise to you." Agatha was staring at Twitchett with narrowed eyes. She wasn't even looking at the sack.

I could feel the jackalope squirming in the suitcase, but I hoped that Twitchett didn't notice. I couldn't stop staring at that sack.

"That's right."

"And I'm guessing they're the ones that took your stuff? Because all your papers are gone. Office and apartment. Am I right?"

Twitchett trembled. "My papers? Gone? All of—"

"I'll take that as a yes." Man, you have to give it to Agatha. She was relentless. "So why did you warn us about an informant? Was that just a joke?"

"The men in suits weren't my prime consideration, unfortunately." Professor Twitchett cleared his throat. "I was warning you about some . . . other interested parties, let's say."

Yeah, let's say. Let's be as cryptic as possible when we're being chased around town by maniacs. Good idea. But Twitchett wasn't done.

"And I may have . . . well, they may have discovered your involvement. I apologize for that."

Agatha didn't even blink. "You apologize? For what—for being a total idiot? I mean, seriously, if there's a spy, why keep leaving notes in the hall?"

Professor Twitchett turned three shades paler. "Notes? If you received another note, it didn't come from me."

Agatha just goggled at him. "It didn't come from you."

It was good that Agatha could process the important parts so quickly. I was still stuck on the fact that there was someone besides the Suit guys after us.

"No, it didn't." Professor Twitchett shook his head. "I left instructions for care, guidelines—that's all."

"But you're here!" I couldn't be quiet any longer. "The note said zoo at three. Why are you here at the zoo, at three, if the note wasn't from you?"

"On the phone, you said . . ." Twitchett whispered. "You said you wanted to meet at the zoo at three . . ."

All of the blood drained out of his face. I had a feeling mine looked the same way. I couldn't believe we'd all been so stupid.

"So we walked right into a *trap*?" Agatha said shrilly. She turned and stared at me with huge eyes. "It's a trap!"

We both started scanning the area like crazy people, which is pretty much what we were at that point. And that's when we saw them.

Men in suits. Everywhere.

I don't know how we'd missed them before, but they'd definitely been watching us. They'd managed to clear out all of the regular zoogoers and they'd moved into prime positions to catch us. I didn't see a direction that would be safe to run. Apparently my spy skills are just as lousy as everybody else's.

"Give me the Subject, Jeremy. *Now!*" Twitchett said, grabbing my arm and lunging for the suitcase. I yanked my arm away angrily.

"Push off, jerk," I said, shoving Twitchett back as hard as I could. Boy, did he make the wrong move. Nobody pushes me around like that and gets away with it. And I'll tell you, I sure didn't spend the day protecting that little stinker just to dump him in some cruddy sack like a piece of garbage. Reward or no reward, we were out of there.

Twitchett stumbled back, glared around at the men in suits, and then took off running.

I looked at Agatha. "So now what, Einstein?"

She gave a barky laugh. "Now? Meet up afterward at the room. But now, just RUN!" She took off in the opposite direction from Twitchett, her beret slipping back on her head.

I turned to run in a third direction, because I figured if we all split up, they couldn't catch all of us. And that's when I realized I was the lousiest spy of all. Because while I'd been yapping with Twitchett, one of the Suits had crept up behind me. He was only about ten feet away. And he had something in his hand. It was a . . . well, it looked like a flashlight.

"Just give us the suitcase, son. That's all we want." He twitched the flashlight at me, I guess to show that he was willing to use it. Or that he had an itchy trigger finger. Or something.

I picked up the Dora suitcase and hugged it to my chest. Beats me why. All I had to do was give it to them and our problems would be over. But there was something about having some weirdo threatening me with a flashlight that really ticked me off. Call it a bad attitude, but there was no way I was giving that jerk my jackalope. He was going to have to pry that Dora suitcase out of my cold dead hands.

I backed away slowly. Out of the corner of my eye, I could see the other Suits chasing Agatha and Twitchett, and the ones that weren't were too far away to grab me.

I backed up more, carefully though, because I was only a few feet from Señor Slappy's tank. I could hear him back there, barking and splashing. And suddenly I knew exactly what to do. I was going to use my secret weapon.

"Come on now, son. Don't make this hard on yourself." Mr. Suit-with-the-Flashlight was walking slowly toward me with this smarmy smirk on his face, like his getting the jackalope was a sure thing. But that's because he didn't know what I knew. He'd never met Señor Slappy.

I backed up until I felt the metal railing against my back. Then I waited. I could hear Señor Slappy swim over and start going through his routine behind me. Mr. Suit-with-a-Flashlight wasn't even paying attention to him. I just needed to make sure I timed this right.

Mr. Suit-with-a-Flashlight stopped a few feet away and looked at me with pity on his face, like I was a lame-o loser. "Let's just end this, okay, son? Hand it over."

I nodded. Señor Slappy was winding up.

"Sure thing." I bent down like I was going to open the suitcase.

The man smiled. "Good boy." And then Señor Slappy hit him smack in the face with a giant wave of stinky water.

I took off running, because my "I'm opening the suitcase" stance was also my "Get ready for the starter's pistol" stance. I could hear the man shouting behind me, and I couldn't help but grin. Seriously, there's nothing better than deploying your secret sea lion defense system against the Feds. That was before my foot hit part of Señor Slappy's breakfast and I took a header right onto the pavement. Right next to that jerk's flashlight.

It must have fallen out of his hands when he got hit in the face with the water, so I grabbed it and pointed it at him while I scrambled to my feet.

"No!" he said. "Don't, please!" So I did what any kid would've done. I let him have it.

I switched on the flashlight, thinking I would blind him, clunk him on the head, and run. But that was no ordinary flashlight. I'd barely even turned it on before he started to turn green and clapped his hands over his mouth. And swear to God, thirty seconds later he was puking his guts out.

My jaw practically hit the ground. Fortunately, I had enough sense to turn around and take off. Unfortunately, I didn't have enough sense to turn the flashlight off right away, and I'm sorry to say that Twiggy, the zoo's resident giraffe, got a faceful. (She had her head lowered and was gawking at us at the time. Kind of serves her right for rubbernecking.)

I don't know if you've ever seen a giraffe barf, but it's pretty much what you'd expect. Suffice it to say that it's not pretty, and you can literally see it coming, so it's nobody's fault but your own if you don't get out of the way.

I got out of the way.

My Suited friend was not so lucky.

I was actually starting to feel pretty good about myself until I heard the gunshots. Apparently that flashlight wasn't the only weapon Mr. Suit had. I felt something brush past my leg, but I didn't stop, even when I accidentally tripped and dropped the puke flashlight in the bushes. I doubled my pace and ducked through the underpass that separated the zoo from downtown. My chest was ready to burst, but there was no way my legs were going to stop moving. Because if they really had started shooting at us, the whole game had changed.

13.

We Decimate the Minibar

Twenty-four hours ago, my biggest concern was how to get my usual C- on my science project.

Twenty-four hours ago, my favorite jeans weren't what I'd call clean, exactly, but they had exactly zero bullet holes in them.

Twenty-four hours ago, I'd never given more than a passing thought as to whether jackalopes existed. And that passing thought hadn't covered things like A) how long a jackalope can live comfortably in a Dora the Explorer suitcase without freaking out and B) how many bathroom breaks a jackalope needs.

Twenty-four hours ago, I never expected to be hiding from homicidal government agents in a hotel linen closet.

I'm going to kill Professor Twitchett.

I'd run past the tuxedo guys and taken the stairs up to the twelfth floor just in case I was being followed. (Three at a time, too. Well, for the first five flights, anyway. Okay, three flights.) I staggered to the room and collapsed in a sweaty mess against the door. That was when I realized I didn't have a key.

I thought about going back down and asking the check-in lady, but I figured after the whole "Where's my dad" stunt, the last thing I should do was draw more attention to myself. Which is why I'd temporarily taken up residence in the linen closet. I was praying the housekeeping staff was done for the day.

It could've been worse, I guess. It smelled nice and clean, and I'd found the stash of pillow chocolates. So it's not like I would starve or anything. Which was good, considering I had no idea how I was going to get out of this mess.

I unzipped the suitcase a little (making sure to point it away from me, in case Jack came out fighting). But he just poked his head out and looked around.

I offered him a pillow chocolate, but he turned up his nose at it. He seemed to appreciate the thought, though, because he gave a big galumphing hop into my lap, kneaded my stomach with his paws for a second, and then settled down for a nap. Which is not an experience I'd ever expected to have.

We sat that way for a couple of minutes, and then my disposable cell phone went off and ruined the moment. (And almost got me impaled on a pair of antlers. Those jackalopes sure can jump when they're startled.)

"Agatha?" I whispered into the phone. Like it was going to be anybody else. I didn't even know that phone number. I really should've paid more attention when she gave it to me, but when someone's flinging a cell phone at your head, it's easy to overlook details.

"Where are you?" Agatha's voice was tinny.

"Linen closet, twelfth floor."

"Stay put. I'm on my way." She hung up before I could say another word.

I stayed put. So did Jack. We may have even done

some napping. All I know is that hallway light sure was bright when Agatha threw the door open.

"Quick, get in the room!" she barked, shooing me with all her might. I scooped Jack up around the middle and staggered into the hotel room. I didn't even bother putting him in his suitcase; I just draped a washcloth over his head. Nobody saw us, but man, I bet those security tapes were interesting.

Agatha scanned the hallway and then hurried back into the room. She was still in panic mode. I offered her a pillow chocolate and she ate it without even registering what it was. It could've been a piece of scented soap for all she noticed.

"So I figured we needed some more supplies," she said, emptying a drugstore shopping bag. She chucked me a small black duffel bag with a reinforced bottom. "That Dora suitcase has got to go. They'll spot us in a second with that thing."

No argument there. If I never saw Dora the Explorer again it would be too soon.

I chucked Dora at the desk trash can (and whiffed it). "What are we going to do? They shot at me!"

Agatha looked up dismissively. "They didn't shoot at you."

I put my foot on the bed and pointed to the hole in my jeans. "Excuse me. Bullet hole?"

Agatha glanced at it and rolled her eyes. "So you fell and got a boo-boo. They did not shoot at you, okay? It's bad enough without you exaggerating."

I waggled my finger in the bullet hole. "Real bullets, Agatha. The guy had a gun."

"We're kids, Jeremy. They're not going to shoot at kids."

I snorted. Tell that to my jeans.

Agatha ignored the snort and pulled a tiny netbook computer out of the shopping bag.

"Good grief, Agatha, how much shopping did you do?"

"What? It was on sale, and we need it! It's not like the Business Center is safe, and we need to get online.

Besides, I told my dad before my birthday that I needed one. It's not my fault he went for the sweater with the squirrel appliqué instead." Agatha glared at me.

I shrugged. I remembered that sweater. I think Agatha wore it for a grand total of two class periods before the jeering got to be too much for her. I was just glad I wasn't going to be the one explaining a massive credit card bill to my parents.

Agatha fired up the netbook. "The first thing we need to do is find out what we're up against." She glanced over at the jackalope, who was pawing at the minibar and making pathetic "ehn" noises. "What's his problem?"

"He wants some whiskey," I said, taking a bottle out of my pocket. I kind of enjoyed hearing the little guy sing.

"Oh, no," Agatha said. "No whiskey for him. We all need to stay sharp." The jackalope shot her a look that should've incinerated her on the spot. Agatha didn't notice.

I tossed the jackalope a pillow chocolate and he turned his fiery laser eyes on me. I made a sympathetic face, and he turned back to the minibar. "Hey, Agatha, here's an idea."

Agatha didn't look up. "What?"

"Do you think they know it's a jackalope? Because maybe if we just tell them that's what it is, they'll think we're crazy and go away."

Agatha didn't say anything.

"I mean, they're imaginary right? Who'd believe it's a jackalope? And why would they want one anyway?"

Agatha typed on her netbook.

"Agatha?"

"Here we go! Hello, wireless Internet!"

So I'm guessing Agatha wasn't listening. Fine, two can play that game.

I picked at the bullet hole in my jeans like it was the most interesting thing in the world and blatantly ignored her fiddling on the computer. I focused on prying loose a tiny burr that had gotten tangled up in the edge of the hole. I was just pretending to be interested at first, but after a couple of minutes, I frowned and looked closer. That burr was really worked in there. And it was blinking. I'd never seen a burr with a green blinking light in it.

"Agatha?" I said, my voice an octave or two higher than I like it to be. I poked at the burr tentatively with my finger. "Holy crap, Agatha, it's flashing." Call me paranoid, but flashing burrs just scream bad news to me. I grabbed the burr and pulled, but it wouldn't come loose. But that wasn't the worst part. The worst part was that the more I messed with it, the more my fingertip started to go numb.

That's when I decided to completely freak out. "Agatha, get it off!" I squeaked, shoving my pants leg at her. "The burr—I can't get it off! I can't get it off!" Not my finest moment, I'll admit.

"What?" Agatha glared at me and then looked at the hole in my pants leg. Her eyes widened as she looked at the burr.

"That's not a burr, Jeremy. That's a—that's not natural." Her voice sounded normal, but I couldn't help but notice that her hands were trembling. Without a word, she grabbed her bag and came back with a pair of scissors. I held my leg out, like some kind of pathetic flamingo or something. Agatha scrunched her face up in concentration and carefully cut the area around the burr out. Then she dropped it on the floor and smashed the hell out of it with the TV remote.

"That's from them, isn't it?" she said, whacking the remains one last time for good measure. The burr lay scattered in tiny pieces on the floor.

"I told you they shot at me."

Agatha just nodded, but her face was pale.

"So what was that, a tranquilizer or something? It messed up my finger." I sucked on my finger, which was probably not a terrific idea, but seemed to make it better.

"Or a bug or something."

I turned the pieces over with the toe of my shoe. I don't know why I thought someone who has a flashlight that can make you barf would use regular bullets. "Who are these guys? He said they weren't Homeland Security or CIA."

Agatha looked solemn. "Someone worse. KGB? Israeli intelligence? Or maybe Nazis? An international crime syndicate?"

"Or Vulcans?" Just thought I'd throw that out there. I hadn't entirely ruled it out.

Agatha just stared at me, but at least she didn't laugh in my face. "Right. Or . . . Vulcans. I have no idea. But we can find out."

"What did Twitchett call them? Look them up."

Agatha nodded, but she looked distracted. "Yeah, I will, in a sec. But first, I want to know what he said about *us*. Where do you think Twitchett did his bragging? We've got to find out how much they know."

The thought of Twitchett talking about us online made my stomach twist. "Just Google his name. We need to know what he said about us."

Agatha typed his name into the search engine and hit enter. "Oh, crud. This doesn't look good."

"What?" I didn't like the sound of her voice. Like with that one click of the keyboard we were doomed.

"He's been on the Mad Scientists International website."

Call me stupid, but that meant nothing to me. But it sure didn't sound promising. "Mad Scientists? That can't be good."

"Mad Scientists International. It's ironic," Agatha said, then paused. "I hope."

She clicked through to the message board and we hunched over the netbook, going through the archives. Twitchett had been awful chatty for a while there. It was pretty bad.

It started out okay, with Twitchett just talking about Agatha's crazy hybrid ideas. Or, sorry, "Agatha H.'s" ideas. Then after a while he stopped mentioning Agatha and started talking about his awesome new project. And then he was just flat-out bragging about how he'd created a jackalope, but it was secret so no one should tell anyone. What a doofus.

Agatha rolled her eyes. "So great, they basically know everything. Sheesh, did he think he was being anonymous? I mean, forget about the fact that he practically put my full name down, and that he called it a stinking *jackalope* instead of animal hybrid, did he really think that the user name 'ProfFrankenTwitch' was going to keep people from figuring out who he was?"

Knowing Professor Twitchett, probably.

"It looks like nobody was taking him too seriously at first, until this 'GS892-C99' person started posting, asking for details and wanting to meet. Then it looks like Twitchett got nervous and disappeared."

I nodded. "And then there's this guy." I pointed at the screen. "This 'Metalman' guy, telling GS892-C99 that he can produce the jackalope. What's up with that? Are there two jackalopes?"

"Or is that our informant? And who's this loser?" Agatha pointed at another user name, ⌄↓↘↘↕↔▽. "What, are those Wingdings? Who actually uses Wingdings anyway?" She snorted in disgust. "At least Twitchett tried to protect your secret identity, 'Igor.' Like there's anyone else who fits that description.

Too bad he practically said he was leaving the jack-alope with you. Guess we know why everyone's after us, huh?"

"Yeah, I guess." I wished GS892-C99 and Metalman and the Wingding idiot were as lax about their user-names as Professor Twitchett. Somehow knowing that they were out there wouldn't be as bad if I could fig-ure out who they were. "So the Suit guys must be one of them, right? So are the Suit guys the Wingdings?"

Agatha shook her head. "I don't know. What was it Twitchett said? Darpa, right?"

I nodded. He said a heck of a lot of gobbledygook, and I didn't remember half of it. But darpa sounded familiar.

"It's got to be something important. Maybe a government thing?" Agatha gave a nervous glance at the remnants on the floor and started typing. "Has to be, with that kind of technology."

"I'll bet it's on—" I started, but Agatha cut me off.

"If you say Wikipedia, I'll rip your throat out."

I didn't say it. (But I bet it was there.)

Agatha hit enter and then sat staring at the computer. "Oh, no. This is bad."

I peered over her shoulder. "What? What's a darpa?"

Agatha didn't move. "It's a government organization. Those guys, they're from DARPA." She looked at me dramatically.

I have to admit it was kind of a letdown. Here I thought we were being tracked by the big guys. CIA, Homeland Security, Vulcans, that kind of thing. Not some piddly little agency I've never even heard of. It was like finding out that you're being chased by clerks from the Better Business Bureau. I don't even know any movies with DARPA guys as the bad guys. And you know they can't be that scary if they're not even in the movies.

"DARPA," I snorted. "Who the heck are they?"

Agatha cleared her throat. "Well for one, they're military. It's an acronym: It means Defense Advanced Research Projects Agency. It's part of the Defense Department."

Military was definitely scarier than the Better Business Bureau. I frowned and peered closer. Man, do those netbooks have little screens. And Agatha's big head wasn't helping. "That can't be right, though. What would the Defense Department want with Jack?"

"You're right, it doesn't make sense. Maybe he didn't say DARPA." Agatha did another search. "I mean, he's just a—" She froze and looked at me in horror. "Oh, crap." She turned the screen so I could see it.

"What?" I looked at what she'd called up. I was trying to be realistic here. It couldn't be that bad, right? I stared at the screen and then back at Agatha. And then back at the screen. "That can't be right, can it? Does that say—"

"Cyborg moths. It says cyborg moths," Agatha said in a monotone.

I'll admit it. I was like your classic cartoon wolf with my eyes bugging out at the screen. "They're working on cyborg moths?"

Agatha nodded and read from the screen. "Remote-controlled cyborg moths equipped with surveillance equipment. They're implanting chips in their brains as caterpillars. Robot moth spies."

"Oh, of course." I scanned the screen Agatha had up. "Agatha?"

"Yes?"

"Down there, when it says they're developing flesh-eating robots, it doesn't really mean . . ."

"It means flesh-eating robots," Agatha said. "Along with . . ." She peered at the screen. "Invisible self-healing shoot-through shields. And . . . oh yeah. Mind control helmets."

I sat down hard on the red chair. It was that bad.

That little trick Mr. Jones had pulled earlier at my apartment, zapping the power with his pen—that was nothing compared with what he could do. He really had just been playing with me.

"They probably started salivating as soon as they read Twitchett's messages." Agatha read a little more and then shut the netbook. I didn't blame her. There is definitely such a thing as knowing too much. I'd never dreamed we were dealing with people crazier than Twitchett. I'd liked it better when they were just government bad guys in suits.

I stared at the Dora suitcase lying on its side with holes poked in the corners of the fabric. And it all clicked. "Jackalopes are killers, Agatha. That's what it is. When you provoke them, they turn into crazed killers. They're unstoppable."

Agatha nodded gloomily. "That makes sense, then. DARPA must know that. They're the ultimate secret weapon. Nobody would expect you to be packing a crazed angry jackalope. And if they could control them . . ."

We both stared at the suitcase for what seemed like forever. Then Agatha finally straightened up. "Well, fine. We know what we're up against. Now we have to figure out what to do."

I nodded. Except it seemed to me that the only decision was whether we planned to cry or not cry when we went to surrender. Because no matter what Agatha said, I knew it wasn't that easy.

"That's the thing, though. We *don't* know what we're up against, Agatha. We don't have a clue."

Agatha looked confused. "But we do. DARPA guys with guns that shoot tranquilizers. Or bugs or whatever."

I felt like shaking her. "Get real. Those Suit guys? Flunkies. They have to be. If those were the actual DARPA guys, we wouldn't even be having this conversation—we would've woken up this morning wrapped up tight in cybermoth cocoons. As soon as the Suit guys call in the actual big guns, it's all over." We were doomed. "Flesh-eating machines, Agatha. Moth armies. Flashlights that make you puke!"

"Okay." Agatha nodded carefully, like I was a defective firecracker about to go off. I realized I hadn't even told her about the puke ray yet, but to her credit, she didn't call me a wack job. "So we just have to out-wit the Suit guys before they call in the big guns. And you can tell me all about the puking flashlight later on. That's all there is to it." Agatha stood up and made an attempt at a smile. "So where's our furry friend?"

I looked around for Jack and groaned out loud. He wasn't hard to find. He hadn't technically moved, but now he was standing next to a pile of what used to be the minibar. To his credit, he had a really guilty expression on his face (not to mention the shard of metal hanging out of his mouth).

Agatha stared at him blankly. "Is that because I wouldn't let him have whiskey?"

I nodded. I made a mental note to hustle the next time Jack went "ehn." I didn't even know you could shred a little refrigerator like that.

"Well, that's going on the credit card," Agatha said, still completely blank. I think the stress of the day had finally gotten to us. Jack licked his lips, flicking the shard of metal away. (It ended up embedded in the wall nearby.) Then he lazily flopped over on his side.

At least one of us wasn't freaking out.

"You know what'll happen to him if they catch us." Agatha didn't look at me—she just watched Jack lick a paw.

"They'll make him a killer."

"Worse. Experiments. Dissections. They'll need to know how he works so they can make more. Thousands more."

I swallowed hard. "Then they won't catch us."

We watched Jack dozing until the sound of traffic sirens outside snapped us out of our stupor. Agatha picked up the trash can to clean up the remains of the minibar, and I went to the window and peered down at the street. There were military Humvees and long black cars blocking the road at either end of the block. Not a great sign, I didn't think.

"Hey Agatha," I said, craning my neck to get a better look. "That credit card of yours. Whose name did you say is on that, exactly?"

Agatha shrugged and started scooping pieces of minibar into the trash. "Mine. It's legal, okay? I can deal with my dad."

I nodded. "It's not that. I was just trying to figure how fast the Feds could tell you used it. A day or two? Or an hour?"

Agatha went pale and dropped the trash can. "Why, you don't think—"

Then the hotel phone rang.

We both stared at it in horror. There was no reason for anyone to be calling us. Nobody knew we were here. And I really didn't think the front desk could've found out about the minibar yet.

"Should we answer it?" Agatha said.

"I don't know."

Agatha drifted over to the phone like a sleepwalker and stared at it, the flashing red phone light shining on her face. Then she picked it up. "Hello?"

She stood listening for a second, and then put it down.

"There's no one there."

We stared at each other without moving for a few long seconds. I swallowed hard. "That burr," I said, forcing my voice to work. "Maybe it wasn't a bug. Maybe it's a tracker."

It was like someone flipped a switch. Agatha lunged for the netbook and her bookbag, and I lunged for the jackalope, stuffing him in the duffel bag in a way that I'm sure he really didn't appreciate.

Then we took off down the hall.

"Stairs! They'll be watching the elevators," Agatha gasped as we hurried into the stairway, slamming the door behind us. Then we stopped short. Because it was just like being in a gym pool. The acoustics were awesome. Which would've been fine, except that meant anything we said, any movement we made, would be heard by anyone on any other floor. Anyone hiding, waiting for us to come blundering by. We had to creep.

Creeping down twelve flights of stairs isn't really something I'd recommend. Especially at the Grand Empyrean, because the stairs are marble and cold and murder on the knees. I wouldn't give it more than one star.

It felt like it took hours, crawling stair by stair, but we finally got to the ground floor. We crept up to the door, creaking and hobbling like senior citizens, and peered out into the lobby. They definitely knew we were there.

Suit guys were watching the front doors and talking to the tuxedo guys, making those doors doubly impossible to get through. More Suit guys were talking to the front desk people, and random other Suits were milling around in the indoor trees. We were stuck.

"Front door's out," Agatha said. "Side door, you think?"

"Maybe . . ." I hesitated, hoping that I would see some opening that we could take advantage of. But all I could see were the Suit guys, a few stray hotel guests, and some little kid sucking on the hem of her Disney Princesses shirt.

And then I knew what to do.

I have to take a minute to say thank you to the kid in the Disney Princesses shirt for being my source of inspiration. Because you can't watch as many crappy Disney movies as I have without knowing the perfect way to escape. I elbowed Agatha in the ribs. "Not the side door. Kitchen." I pointed at the Disney Princesses kid. "Okay? Kitchen." I raised my eyes meaningfully.

She grinned at me. Apparently she'd seen as many crappy Disney movies as I have.

We counted to three and then took off running for the kitchen. Okay, so if you haven't seen a lot of crappy

Disney movies, let me explain. First off, I'm talking the live-action ones that are super old, the ones that my mom's always bringing home from the library and bribing me to watch. In every single one of those, there's the big chase scene through the kitchen, where someone knocks over a pot of something slippery, people fall down and slide into big bags of flour, and hilarity ensues. And the people being chased always escape. *Always*.

So that was our goal.

We raced down the hallway away from the entrance, weaved our way through the restaurant, and then slammed through the swinging doors of the kitchen, picking up a tail of Suit guys as we went, just like in a crappy Disney movie.

And after that, it really wasn't much like a crappy Disney movie anymore.

Agatha lunged for a pot on the stove, but she just winged it and only managed to burn her finger. I think she spilled maybe two drops. I knocked an empty pan onto the floor, but instead of getting angry and charging us, the kitchen guys mostly just stared. If the pan I knocked down hadn't tripped one of the Suit guys, it would've been a total waste.

We burst out into the street and then turned and ran blindly to the left, away from the blockade. The pathetic thing was, there was really no point in running at all. There was no way we were going to escape, no matter what happens in movies. There were only two of us, and lots of them, and we're not that fast.

The kitchen door slammed open behind us. I didn't look back, but I knew it was only a matter of seconds before their hands would be on our shoulders.

And then, just as my legs were about to give out, I heard a huge squealing sound and Bob the lab assistant drove up onto the curb in front of us, van door hanging open.

"GET IN!" screeched in his reedy voice. Me and Agatha didn't even hesitate. We jumped in and slammed the door just as the Suit guys caught up to the van. Bob hit the automatic door locks, peeled out, and took off down the street.

I grabbed my seat belt to buckle up and shoved a photo lying on the seat out of the way. I frowned and took a closer look. It was a photo of me and Twitchett, grainy and taken from a long way away. I was handing him a bag (probably of Preparation H).

And that's when I realized what we'd done.

We'd gotten into Bob's van. His white van. And suddenly I knew what had been bugging me about Bob. In the lab, when I met Bob for the very first time? He kept asking me, "What do you think about this, Jeremy? Jeremy, what do you think about that?"

But I'd never met Bob before. Bob shouldn't have known my name.

14.

Quality Time with Bob

Agatha crawled into the front seat of the van. "Wow, Bob, where'd you come from? Good timing, huh?" Agatha looked over her shoulder and grinned at me. She hadn't put it all together yet.

I tightened the grip on Jack's duffel bag and slowly reached out to try the door handle. I'd heard about people doing that rolling jump thing out of a moving car, and I was willing to give it a try. How hard could it be? Well, harder than it looks, apparently, especially when you're in a stupid passenger van with child safety locks.

I slumped back in my seat to figure out a Plan B. Bob was staring at me in the rearview mirror.

"I control the locks, Jeremy," Bob said casually.

"Yeah, I figured." I glared out of the window. I couldn't stand looking at Bob's weaselly face, and I was ticked that I'd given myself away.

Agatha turned around in her seat and stared back at me. Somebody needed a whack with the cluestick. "What's going on?"

"Why don't you ask your good friend Bob here?" I said, glaring back at Bob.

Agatha turned and frowned at Bob. "What the heck. Bob?"

Bob laughed and reached out to tousle her hair, but she ducked away. "Beats me. Sounds like somebody needs a nap. Right, Jeremy?"

"Yeah, about that. Who told you my name?" Why beat around the bush? It's not like I was going anywhere. I might as well lay it all out.

Bob didn't answer, but Agatha twisted around and stared at me for a long minute. I reached over and propped up the photo so she could see it.

Agatha's eyes widened, then without a word, she

sat back in her seat and adjusted her bookbag in her lap. Whacking complete.

"So, how did you know Jeremy's name?" she said, trying to sound casual. But it had gone up by about an octave. "Did Professor Twitchett tell you about him? Or did I do it and just forget?"

"Yeah, that's it. One of those." Bob chuckled.

"That's what I figured." Agatha gave a weird unnatural laugh and then cleared her throat. "So thanks a ton, Bob. You really saved our hide back there. But you can just drop us at the corner. We've got a thing. You know. At the place. We've got to go."

I nodded. "That's right. Wish we could explain, but . . ." I shrugged.

Bob's eyes darted over to Agatha for a second and then he tightened his grip on the steering wheel. "I don't think so, Agatha."

"No, it's okay. Just anywhere is fine." I could see her knuckles turning white as she gripped her bookbag.

"Why don't you give me what's in the bag, Agatha?" Bob's voice was cold.

Agatha froze. "What? This bag?"

"Just give it to me, Agatha!" Bob barked and then caught himself. "Don't play games with me."

Agatha's eyes were huge, but she gave a half shrug. "Sorry, Bob. You're too smart for me. I'm totally busted." She hesitated and then unzipped her backpack. And then she slowly pulled out the netbook. "You're right, I shouldn't have bought it. But if you really want it . . ."

"I'm not stupid, Agatha," Bob said, all friendliness gone from his voice. "I know about Twitchett's project. I took your notebook."

"You took . . ." The muscles in Agatha's jaw started working, like she was gearing up for something big, but Bob cut her off.

"So it's in the duffel bag, Jeremy? Is that where it is?" Bob glared at me in the rearview mirror.

"Whatever," I shrugged, staring out of the window. I wasn't even going to participate in the conversation. Anything that distracted me from figuring a way out of the van wasn't worth my time. So far all I could come up with was the strangle-Bob-while-he's-driving option,

199

and since I didn't want this to end in a fiery car crash, I eliminated it as an option. (Reluctantly.)

"Don't make this hard on yourself, Agatha. Tell Jeremy to hand over the duffel bag."

I tightened my grip but kept staring out of the window.

"But you're my friend!" Agatha said. She really sounded betrayed. That'll teach her to pal around with creepy hipster types.

"Agatha, you're just a kid. This is my career." Bob shook his head. "You'll understand when you're older, okay?"

"Yeah, right," Agatha muttered, giving him a black look and launching into a tirade of her choicest bad words.

Bob swerved and almost went into the ditch at the side of the road. Apparently Bob wasn't expecting his mother's family line to be called into question. I guess he didn't know Agatha as well as he thought.

Bob said a few cusswords himself, and then his jacket pocket started to vibrate and sing that oldies song, "Highway to Hell." He fumbled for his cell phone and answered it. I've never heard a more appropriate ring tone.

"Yeah," Bob said, looking at us nervously while he drove with one hand. If I was going with my strangle-Bob-while-he's-driving plan, this would be the perfect time for it. But I just glared at him. Yeah, I'm really tough.

Agatha turned around and jerked her head toward Bob. "Metalman," she mouthed.

I nodded. Crap. She was right.

"I got them. Yeah, the kids. They're in the van." Bob shot us a threatening look. "What? They were right there! I couldn't just . . . Look, what was I supposed to . . . Okay, I'm bringing them to . . . No! I'm bring—fine. Fine." Bob slammed his phone back into his pocket, and did an abrupt U-turn, whacking me and Agatha against the doors.

"Change of plans," Bob said. "You're going to see the boss."

I rolled my eyes. How corny can you get? *You're going to see the boss*. But I had a terrible feeling in the pit of my stomach, like I was getting an ulcer or was going to puke or something. Agatha stopped cussing and got a stricken look on her face.

I tried the door handle again. Still locked. I felt so useless, especially since I don't even know how to successfully strangle anybody.

We sat in silence while Bob tore down the highway and then stopped and parked the car. Directly in front of our building.

Agatha and I exchanged glances. Bob had definitely made a big miscalculation, bringing us right to our own apartments. I was pretty sure at least one of us would be able to make a break for it. And come on, I haven't been able to get inside the building without at least one of the nosy neighbors spotting me the entire time I've lived there.

Bob switched off the car and turned to look at us. "Now I'm only going to say this once, okay? We're going inside and I expect complete and total cooperation from you two. Got it?"

I curled my lip at him. What a joke.

Bob nodded at me. "I thought you might feel that way. So you might like to see this."

He opened his jacket. Inside, he had a huge, long hunting knife strapped into the lining. One of those big ones, the kind that can take apart a grizzly bear in a couple of swipes. I swallowed hard and tried to act cool.

Bob closed his jacket. "Now we're going to take your bags and go inside, and you're not going to scream, you're not going to run, you're not going to do a thing except say, 'Hello, Mom,' or 'Hi, Mrs. Garcia,' if we run into anyone. Because I'll use this knife if I have to. On you, or on your families if you get away. And I will do it. Are we clear on this?" Bob watched us, and his face was cold. It hit me hard, right then. He really didn't care at all what happened to us. He'd just as soon kill us.

We got out of the van slowly, and Bob came around and grabbed me by the arm. He may be wiry and scrawny looking, but that guy really is strong. "Don't make this difficult, Jeremy," he hissed at me.

He jerked me around to Agatha's side of the van, waited while she got out, and marched us into the building. It was all a blur. I couldn't believe I was just walking along with him, doing nothing. Here's my chance to be a big hero, escape, and save the day and instead all I do is act like a pathetic puppy on a leash. I saw on *Oprah* once that if someone grabs you, you're not supposed to let them take you to a second location. But I just kept walking. I guess my feet hadn't watched *Oprah*.

Bob's hand on my arm was acting like a tourniquet, cutting off all the blood. It was all I could focus on. I glanced over at Agatha. She looked as embarrassed and horrified as I felt.

I didn't even really register where we were going until I heard Agatha gasp. I looked up just as Bob shoved us through the door into Mrs. Simmons' apartment.

15.

Let There Be Blood

"Mrs. Simmons?" I gasped as the door slammed behind us.

Agatha cursed softly under her breath. "I need to learn to read Wingdings."

Mrs. Simmons was sitting on one of her dining room chairs, directly across from the door. She had a handgun in her lap and was smoking a cigarette. She didn't have that spacey-old-lady look she usually did—it was like somebody had come in with a file and sharpened her entire face. I wouldn't even have recognized her on the street.

And she looked angry. Really angry. At Bob.

"This is not what I told you to do, Bob," she said, tapping ash from her cigarette onto the floor. "The suitcase, Bob. The suitcase, not the brats."

Well, that stung. Agatha actually flinched. We'd never been anything but nice to Mrs. Simmons, even if she was crazy as a loon. (To her face, anyway.)

Bob swallowed hard. "Yeah, but see, they came running out of the hotel with the DARPA agents after them, and I saw they had two bags, so I figured . . . "

"You figured, Bob? You figured you'd blow both your cover and mine on the *chance* they had the project?" She ground her cigarette out on the carpet and got up.

"What was your job, Bob? Do you remember?" She dangled the handgun from one hand and strolled over to him.

"Watching the kids," Bob said.

"*Watching* the kids. Not *snatching* the kids."

I didn't like that gun one bit. I wouldn't have liked it if the old Mrs. Simmons had it, but with the new Mrs. Simmons it was even worse. Old Mrs. Simmons might have blown your head off, but at least it would've been an accident.

"But I was so close! My note to get them to come to the zoo? They never suspected it was from me! If it wasn't for Twitchett and those damn agents, they would've handed it over to me, no questions asked."

I should've known better than to trust some blurry note. I'd been so stupid all along.

Mrs. Simmons pressed her lips together in a tight smile. "I was getting information, Bob. They were confiding in me. They trusted me. We would have had it, Bob, if you hadn't *blown our cover*."

"I'm sorry," Bob said so softly I almost couldn't hear him.

"You did, didn't you, Jeremy. Trust me." She came over and squeezed my face with her hand. "You almost left your little secret with me earlier today. So close . . ." She gave my face one last hard squeeze and then motioned to the duffel bag with the gun.

"Open it."

I put the duffle bag on the ground. There was no Señor Slappy behind me to rescue me now. No secret weapon to save the day this time. I hadn't even managed to hold on to the barf flashlight. I just hoped Jack would forgive me.

I unzipped the bag and stood back.

It took a minute before the jackalope poked his head out and looked around the room. Pretty typical stuff for me and Agatha, but big excitement for Mrs. Simmons and Bob. Bob gasped out loud and Mrs. Simmons gave a tiny squeal of glee, the kind a rabid squirrel might make.

Jack shook his head, pretty much shredding the edges of the duffel bag with his antlers, hopped out onto the floor, and looked around. Then he hurried into the corner of the room, turned around, and glared at us.

He had his tough face on, but I could tell he was a little freaked out, mostly because he left a trail of freaked out on his way to the corner.

"You realize what you have here, Jeremy?" Mrs. Simmons said to me, her eyes glittering.

"Uh, yeah. It's uh . . ." I looked at Agatha. "An animal hybrid. A mixture of the . . . the DNA of a bunny and some kind of . . . deer?" I looked at Agatha, and she nodded with this weird proud look on her face.

"No, stupid boy. What you have here is a jackalope."
Mrs. Simmons turned her back on me in disgust.

I cleared my throat. "No, see, jackalopes are imaginary. This is a hybrid—"

Mrs. Simmons whirled around. "It is one of the rarest and deadliest creatures known to man. Do you know the damage these can do? The destruction?"

Well, in a word, yeah. I saw the minibar.

"One jackalope is almost unstoppable. A heartless, ruthless killing machine. Can you imagine what an *army* of these killers could do? The world would be forced to its knees, Jeremy. Forced to obey whoever controls them."

The jackalope stood in the corner and blinked his long lashes at us.

"Armies of little guys like him?" I heard what she was saying, but it was hard to imagine. I'd just spent the day with Jack, and I know that was his rep, but he didn't seem like a killer to me. Sure, he was a little destructive, but that wasn't really his fault. It was the antlers, mostly. Still, the idea of a whole army of Jacks, angry because they didn't get their whiskey . . .

"Whole cities could be wiped out, Jeremy. It's not just an amusing curiosity or a *pet*." She spit the word out like it was obscene. "I understand this. The government understands this. Why do you think those agents want him so much, Jeremy? Twitchett gave them no choice when he refused to play ball. What do you think would happen if one of our enemies controlled this secret? A creature like this is too deadly for them *not* to have. Twitchett was just too much of a fool to recognize this golden opportunity."

"So you're going to give him to them?" Agatha said, sounding really small. "DARPA? The Suit guys?"

Mrs. Simmons laughed. "DARPA? DARPA turned its back on me years ago. They've had their chance. No, I'll give him to whoever pays the biggest price, Agatha. I work for myself. I'll teach them to underestimate Gloria Simmons."

Jack stomped a tufty little paw and twitched his fluffy cottony tail.

Mrs. Simmons watched him and frowned.

I tried to laugh. "Wow, Agatha, we're pretty lucky he didn't kill us. Who knew something so cute could be a killer?"

Jack blinked his Disney cartoon eyes and twitched his long silky whiskers.

Mrs. Simmons' frown got deeper. "You did something to him, didn't you?" She turned to face me. She didn't look happy. (Not that she ever looked happy, but even less happy than usual.) "You gave him whiskey, didn't you?"

"What? Why would we do that?" I stammered. We were so busted.

"You idiots, you've tamed him! Destroyed his killer instinct forever! No wonder he's acting so docile. Give a jackalope whiskey and he's putty in your hands; everybody knows that. Morons." Mrs. Simmons spit at us in disgust, her hand tightening on the gun. "A Beanie Baby's more dangerous now."

I tried to ignore her. Because, excuse me, everybody doesn't know that. It's not like that Beanie Baby stuff's common knowledge. It doesn't say a thing about it on Wikipedia.

Mrs. Simmons waved the gun at Jack. "Bob, go get the jackalope. They've ruined him with alcohol."

"Does that mean no money?" Bob sounded nervous. Yeah, I know, what else is new?

"Of course not—not as long as we're the only ones who know. He's still a jackalope, even if he is a wimp. Now go get him. We're leaving. Just as soon as we dispose of these two."

I felt cold all over. I didn't like her tone. And I didn't like the significant look Mrs. Simmons was shooting Bob. Especially since I thought that "dispose of us" probably meant exactly what it sounded like.

Bob wiped his hands on his jeans and hurried over to Jack, who was licking a paw with his delicate pink tongue. He looked up at Bob and drew back a little in fear.

Bob lunged at him. And then all hell broke loose.

You know that crazed killer thing? And that slashy antler stuff? Man, they weren't kidding. I'll never doubt Wikipedia again. I had to close my eyes, that's how bad it was. We're talking blood and screaming and gunshots and chunks of things flying around. (I found out later it was pieces of chair cushion, but at the time I thought it was pieces of Bob.) It seemed to go on forever. I reached out and grabbed onto Agatha and we just clung together, hoping that we'd still be in one piece when we opened our eyes.

A huge crashing noise drowned out the screams, and I opened my eyes just in time to see Mr. Jones and the other Suits burst into the apartment. And Jack run out.

If I never see another gun in my life it'll be too soon. Because all of the Suits had them, and they were pointing them all at Mrs. Simmons and Bob. To be honest, though, I didn't see the point. It was pretty obvious those two weren't going anywhere. It's hard to make a good clean getaway when you're lying in a pool of blood.

I have to hand it to Jack—he'd done a really good job of making it a gorefest without doing any permanent damage, as far as I could tell. What I mean is that Bob and Mrs. Simmons both seemed to still have all of their parts. But they were scratched and slashed within an inch of their lives.

"Step back, son," Mr. Jones said to me as he hauled Mrs. Simmons up and handcuffed her.

I looked back at the door, where Suit guys were milling in and out and talking into their cuffs. None of them seemed to realize that the jackalope they were all after had just left the scene. Or that all their milling in and out had wiped away the tiny bloody pawprints lead-ing into the hallway. And I sure as heck wasn't going to tell them.

I stopped clinging to Agatha; not that she even noticed. She looked traumatized and horrified, but she gave a quick head jerk toward the door when she caught my eye. I nodded. Then we just watched as the Suit guys hauled Bob and Mrs. Simmons toward the door.

One of the Suits had a big flashlight strapped to his belt. I nudged Agatha and pointed. "Puke ray."

The man raised an eyebrow at me, and with one smooth motion, flipped the flashlight out of its holder and held it out to me. "Want to do the honors, kid?" he said, nodding at Bob.

It was a tempting offer, but I didn't trust myself with one of those things. I still felt too guilty about Twiggy. I shook my head. He just chuckled, reholstered the flashlight, and led Bob out of the building.

Mr. Jones disappeared into the kitchen and came out with a dish towel. He was wiping the blood off his hands as he came over toward us. Really gross, if you ask me.

"What, no thank you?" He wasn't smiling.

"Thank you," I said. I meant it, too. Whether I'd still mean it in five minutes, I wasn't sure.

"Those two won't be causing any more trouble. We've been tracking them for quite a while." He shot Agatha a half grin. "Her user name was just her last name in Wingdings 3. Doesn't take much to break a code like that."

Agatha gave a crazed giggle. We were both still pretty wound up.

"So now we come to the big question. Where is it?"

Mr. Smith tossed the dish towel onto Mrs. Simmons' chair and folded his arms. He looked like he expected us to magically pull a jackalope out of his ear or something.

I shook my head. "I don't know." It was nice to be able to tell the truth for a change (or at least part of it).

Mr. Jones looked disappointed in us. You know, that "I'm not angry" kind of disappointed. "Are you really starting that again? We just saved your hide, Jeremy."

I shook my head. "No, really. I don't know where it is."

"We really don't," Agatha said.

Mr. Jones stared at us and then went over to the door and started arguing with Mr. Suit #2.

"He went out into the hall, did you see?" Agatha whispered, never taking her eyes off of Mr. Jones.

"I know." I kept expecting screams or something to come from the entryway, but there wasn't anything. No sounds of carnage. No jackalope attack.

Mr. Suit #2 started talking into his cuff and Mr. Jones came back over to us. He was smiling this time. He'd apparently decided on a new tactic.

"This has been a trying day for all of us. But I think you two owe me one." He paused. "You realize, of course, that Simmons would never have left you alive. Now, where is it?"

We didn't say anything. Agatha just stared at the floor. I glanced over at the door, where Mr. Suit #2 was still talking to his cuff. And I saw a tiny flash of cottony tail disappear down the hall. I quickly jerked my head up to look at the ceiling. I didn't want to do anything to give Jack away.

Mr. Jones leaned forward. "Just so we're straight. We're talking about the jackalope. We know what it is. We know you had it. We know what it did here in the apartment. It's a dangerous killer, Jeremy. Unpredictable. A wild animal."

I kept staring at the ceiling as he talked, and then it was like the cobwebby light fixture had sent me a message. I knew what to do.

I looked Mr. Jones full in the face. "Mrs. Simmons was lying. He wasn't here. The jackalope I mean. We don't have him. But we can get him. We know where he is."

Agatha looked at me in horror.

Mr. Jones smiled encouragingly. "That's good, Jeremy."

"Mrs. Simmons and Bob started fighting over who was going to take us to get him. With that." I pointed at Bob's hunting knife, which had come loose when his jacket was being slashed to ribbons. It was lying in a puddle of blood, so it definitely looked like it could've been what caused all the slashes. "But the jackalope, we only had him before we got here. They took him away from us and stashed him someplace. He wasn't ever here, not as far as I know."

Mr. Jones nodded. "Fine. That's fine. But you'll take me to get him now. Won't you?"

I took a deep breath and avoided Agatha's eyes. "Right."

"What? Jeremy!" Agatha whacked me on the arm.

"No, Agatha, it's the only thing to do. Except . . ." I looked at Mr. Jones, trying to make my face look as innocent as possible. "We don't actually know where he is right this second. We can get him, but not until tomorrow. But I promise—we'll hand him over then. At school, in the gym. Four o'clock."

Mr. Jones' eyes narrowed. "This isn't a negotiation. You're taking me to the jackalope *now*."

"No, really, I wish we could, but we can't right now. We only know where he'll be tomorrow at four, I swear. You just need to give us a chance to get him. We can't until then." I held my breath. I didn't know what to do if he didn't go for it. Especially since I really didn't have any idea where the jackalope was now.

"You realize you're forcing me to arrest you." Mr. Jones sighed and shook his head. Then he reached in his pocket.

I'd seen enough DARPA gadgets to last me a lifetime, so I didn't even want to know what he was getting ready to do to us. I gave it one last-ditch effort. "He trusts us—if we try to rush things it'll just mess everything up."

Mr. Jones frowned at me, like he was reading something written on my forehead. I held my breath.

Mr. Suit #2 stopped talking into his cuff and motioned toward Mr. Jones. "It's Twitchett! They've got a lock on him. They need you!"

Mr. Jones hesitated, glaring at us.

"Jones! You want to explain how you lost him a second time?" Mr. Suit #2 barked.

Mr. Jones grabbed me by the shirt front. "Four o'clock. But know this. You will produce the jackalope. You will hand it over. And if you fail to do so at that time, you will be taken into custody, your parents will be taken into custody, and everything will become evidence in your trial for treason. Am I clear?"

I nodded. Agatha just gaped at me. Mr. Jones shoved me away and hurried after Mr. Suit #2.

"Wait, what about Professor Twitchett?" I said. He was the one person who could spoil my whole plan. "Did you catch him?"

Apparently Twitchett was a touchy subject, because a ticked-off look flashed across Mr. Jones' face. "Your Professor Twitchett boarded a plane to Venezuela this afternoon. We've got agents tracking his movements.

Make no mistake, I'll get him." He didn't look pleased, though. "Four o'clock," he said deliberately, and then turned and left.

Agatha waited until he was gone to turn on me. "What the heck, Jeremy? Are you insane?" She was doing that spitting thing again. I think she does it when she gets really mad. (Something she has in common with Jack, actually.)

I could tell I was going to have to do some serious explaining. "Look, Agatha. It's the only way. You know they're not going to leave us alone, not ever. Not as long as they know about Jack."

"But four o'clock? Are you crazy? That's the science fair!" Agatha hissed.

"I know." I looked around. Mr. Suit #2 was still in the doorway, but it didn't look like he could hear us. "Listen, I've got an idea. It's our only shot."

"If you're so ready to hand him over, why wait? Why not do it right now?" Agatha glared at me.

"Because we need time to set things up." I leaned forward, and with one eye on Mr. Suit #2, I told her my plan. I have to admit, though, she didn't seem to think it was the foolproof work of genius that I thought it was. In fact, she seemed to think it was pretty lame.

"You're not serious." Agatha stared at me like I was completely brain-dead.

"Well, yeah, actually, I am."

"You can*not* think that will work." She had a look on her face like she'd just taken off in an airplane and then realized the pilot was a chipmunk.

But, yeah, I thought it would work. Well, might work. It had a chance. I don't want to get into percentages here.

I raised one eyebrow. "You'd rather do electricity with a potato?"

Agatha sagged. It was a cheap shot, I know.

"Think about Twitchett. Think about what they know about him. It'll work." I smiled. "Two words — baboon butts."

Agatha gave me the ghost of a smile. "Okay, I'm in," she said, just as Mr. Suit #2 came over.

"Hey, you two. You need to clear out. Now." He picked up Agatha's backpack, went through it quickly, and handed it to her. "Here, take your stuff."

Agatha went over and took her backpack. I didn't take anything. Like I needed the remnants of a shredded duffel bag.

"Hey, don't forget this." Mr. Suit #2 picked up a notebook with PROPERTY OF AGATHA written in elaborate bubble letters on the front and handed it to her.

Agatha's eyes got wide. "Thanks," she gushed, clutching it to her chest. I tried to catch her eye, but she didn't even notice. Somebody was still riding the freakout train.

She hurried out into the hallway and let herself into her apartment. I hung back and watched as Mr. Suit #2 put up police tape, went into Mrs. Simmons' apartment, and locked the door. Then I followed her in.

I glanced at my watch. It was just about time for our parents to start getting home. This had to be the longest day of my life.

"So now we wait?" Agatha said.

"Just until most of the Suits are gone."

We sat in Agatha's window, watching the Suit activity until it looked like only Mr. Suit #2 was still there. Then we crept back out into the hallway. We had to get this done before our parents got home from work, or we were totally screwed.

I put one of Agatha's saucers on the floor and poured a little of the hotel whiskey into it. "Hey!" I whispered. "Jack!"

Even with Agatha standing guard, I was convinced that Mr. Suit #2 was going to come out and bust us at any second, or Mrs. Garcia was going to come downstairs and scream. And I didn't even want to think about what would happen if Jack had lost his taste for whiskey.

I sat back on my heels in the hallway, waiting for a glimpse of twitchy nose or fluffy tail, but there was nothing. No sign of him.

Agatha and I exchanged worried looks. "They'll be getting home soon." she whispered. "Hurry!"

I poured a little more whiskey in the dish and waved my hand over it, trying to make the smell float around. Which was really going to be fun to explain to my parents. I had a feeling that I smelled like a distillery.

"Jack!" I whispered again. Nothing.

Then, just when I was feeling desperate, I heard it.

"He went that way!" A tiny voice came from under the stairs. It sounded just like Professor Twitchett.

"Did you hear that?" Agatha said, looking around.

"Jack?" I said a little more loudly. I waved my hand over the whiskey again.

"Quick, over there!" The voice under the stairs came again, but this time it sounded like Bob.

I looked nervously at Mrs. Simmons' door. "Come on, Jack."

I clinked the bottle against the dish, and at the sound, Jack gave a skittery jump out into the hallway. He had blood on his antlers and matted into his fur. He looked pretty rough, but I've never seen a jackalope look more awesome. I pretended not to notice the crazy in his eyes. Jack wouldn't hurt me. I had to believe that.

I pushed the dish closer to him. "Want some?" I was trying to act casual, but it was hard to ignore the blood dripping onto the floor.

Jack eyed me warily and then hopped over to the dish to do some major-league guzzling. He was definitely a jackalope in need of a pick-me-up.

When he was finished boozing it up, I reached down and carefully scooped him up. He snuggled back into my hands and watched me sleepily. I really appreciated him not ripping my throat out.

Agatha hurried over and wiped off his antlers and fur with a tissue.

"You know what to do?" I asked her, holding him out to her.

Agatha nodded and took him from me. "Say good-bye, Jack."

I ruffled him on the head between the antlers. "See you, buddy."

Jack belched affectionately in my face. I would've appreciated it more if it hadn't been as loud as a foghorn.

Agatha jerked the little boozer close to her chest and rushed into her apartment with a grin. She closed the door just as Mr. Suit #2 opened the door and looked out into the hallway.

I waved at him and headed upstairs, looking a whole lot cockier than I felt. I just hoped we would be able to pull this off. Our whole lives depended on it.

16.

Mr. Jones Hates Science

If I thought the rest of the day was going to be relaxing and easy, boy, was I wrong.

I barely had time to change clothes and wash the blood off before my dad got home and whisked me off to buy Styrofoam balls and paint for my model of the planets. (I don't even want to get into the whole Pluto fight we had in the car. The way I see it, if it's officially been declared a nonplanet, it doesn't deserve a spot in my project. My dad's what I would call a Pluto sympathizer, and was of the opinion that I was trying to get out of doing more work. He was right, but that was beside the point.)

The whole apartment building was buzzing about Mrs. Simmons and Professor Twitchett by the time we got back, and by "whole apartment building" I basically mean my parents, the Garcias, and Agatha's mom. (That flight attendant lady was, no surprise, off on a trip somewhere.) Apparently the Garcias had decided to use their cookies for evil, and had weaseled a twisted version of the story out of the Suits who had come back to follow up. They had to come up with something to explain the blood in the hallway. Thankfully, it was a version that didn't include me or Agatha. (From what I heard, it included a sordid love triangle, chemical weapons, illegal zoo animals, and mail fraud.)

And Mrs. Garcia didn't do me any favors by taking the opportunity to talk to my parents about the problems I might be having in school, what with kids picking on me and slashing up my backpack and stealing my books. That kind of thing. Thanks a lot, Mrs. Garcia. I had to do a lot of fancy footwork to get out of that conversation, especially since Mom had discovered the shredded gym suit in my hamper.

So by the time I'd spray-painted my last planet (Pluto. Don't say it.) and stuck them all on the wires, my eyes weren't even open anymore. I don't know how I managed to drag myself to school on time the next morning.

Just in case you were wondering, Agatha and I are both under police surveillance for our drug trafficking and embezzlement scheme. We're going to be arrested as soon as the judge approves the warrant, which could be any time. Or, at least, that's what I overheard in the locker room, so the details may not be 100 percent accurate. And it turns out some kids don't like sharing a classroom with suspected felons, especially when the Feds are supposedly planning to arrest their classmates as accessories. So you can imagine how fun the day was. Especially since there was a giant doomsday clock hanging over my head ticking down to four o'clock.

Agatha had it worse, though. At least a couple of the guys seemed to think that being a federally wanted embezzler and hit man was kind of cool. But the girls basically looked at Agatha like she was a zombie freak (the lack of sleep wasn't doing her any favors either).

I tried to catch her in the hallway between classes to make sure we were all set for four o'clock, but she just gave me a weak smile and drifted away. Carter Oliver saw the whole thing and couldn't keep the smirk off of his face. I hoped that his invisible fish would jump up and rip his face off during the science fair. (Not likely, I know. But I'd pay to see that.)

To tell the truth, I was starting to have bad feelings about my whole plan. Mostly because of Agatha. She had a lot more to lose than I did. If I crashed and burned, nobody would notice, but Agatha's whole reputation as a brainiac was likely to be trashed. And it was too late to do anything about it. Although the truth was that if the plan didn't work, we'd be spending the rest of our lives in the federal pen, so our reputations wouldn't matter anyway. But somehow knowing that didn't make me feel better.

Because before I knew it, it was four o'clock.

If Mr. Jones thought he was going to be meeting us in an empty gym at four, he was sadly mistaken. Because four o'clock was the official beginning of the Buckram County Junior High School Science Fair.

I'd been to the gym earlier to set up my project, and Agatha's was already over in the corner, covered with a sheet. I set mine up next to hers, which would've been project suicide any other time, since her project would just highlight the lameness of mine. Not to mention the damage hanging out with Agatha would've done to my rep. But that stuff just didn't matter anymore.

So at four o'clock we were all lined up in the gym, standing behind our projects, waiting for the judges to make their way down the line. Judging this year was Principal Turner, as usual; Mrs. Marlowe, the science teacher; and school board chair Bitsy Perkins, also known as Carter's mother's real estate partner. Because Buckram County Junior High School is nothing if not impartial.

Agatha was standing next to her project when I got there, looking nervous and chewing on the end of her braid. (Barf.)

I punched her lightly on the shoulder. "We all good?"

She stopped chewing and shrugged. "We're going to jail. Is that good?"

Way to be positive. I lifted the sheet a tiny bit and peeked at the cage underneath. Everything looked good to me. I gave Agatha the thumbs-up.

Agatha glared at me and eyed my project. "You realize Pluto's not a planet, right?"

"Don't start, Agatha."

Agatha started chewing again.

At the front of the room, Principal Turner had gotten out the megaphone and was calling everyone to attention. It would have been more effective if she'd moved the megaphone an inch farther away from her mouth, but we all got the gist of what she was saying. So what if she sounded like one of the grown-ups in those Charlie Brown cartoons?

The judges started at the opposite end of the room, going through the projects one at a time and taking extensive notes. I'd gotten a look at some of the other projects, so I wasn't surprised that they seemed to be zipping right along. Trust me, there wasn't a lot there that you'd want to spend any time on.

Keisha Albright's project was the biggest attention getter. She'd lugged Killer's dream house in, and it was like a fluorescent pink beacon on the other side of the room. She'd gotten it set up with plumbing and taught Killer how to do dishes or something wussy like that. Not that I was looking or anything; I just happened to notice. The judges didn't seem that impressed by it. I have to give Keisha props, though—Killer never lifted a finger to help around the house when he lived with me.

Those judges were staring at the train wreck that was Madison Butler's working model of a gopher's digestive tract when Mr. Jones and his flunkies came into the gym.

They didn't look pleased.

Mr. Jones stopped, scanned the gym, and then zeroed in on us. The look on his face was making me think that maybe I'd made a major miscalculation. I hoped Agatha wasn't right about the whole jail thing. It's pretty much impossible to look cool in a bright orange jumpsuit.

"This wasn't part of our agreement, Mr. Sayle," Mr. Jones said without looking at me. He folded his arms and watched as the judges moved on from the gopher digestion to the reproductive habits of bread mold.

"I know, but . . ."

"It's my whole grade! Please! I've got to beat Carter!" Agatha said in a low, desperate voice. "I know we should've told you, but I had no choice!" It was a moving plea. Heck, I think the lab rats in Dewey Childress' "Watch Rats Get Hopped Up on Sugar Water" project were touched.

Mr. Jones apparently had a heart of stone. "This is not acceptable." He took a step away and started talking into his cuff in a low voice.

Agatha gave me a panicked look, and then jumped forward. "No, wait! Mr. Jones, look, I know you don't want everyone to know about the—" She mouthed the word "jackalope." "But come on, they're not going to believe it anyway, right? And then you can take it. It'll be perfect with your army of cyborg moths."

I stifled a groan. Cyborg moths are just one of those things you don't mention.

Mr. Jones shook her hand off of his sleeve. "This is not a game, Miss Hotchkins. We'll be collecting the Subject now."

He walked back to the entry of the gym, where the other Suits were standing. We didn't have much time if we were going to get away with this.

I took off running down the aisle (at an I'm-not-running pace so I wouldn't get in trouble). Principal Turner and the other judges had just finished scoring Huey Langford's "Ropes: Friends or Foes?" project. (Poor Huey. He needs to get over that rope thing. Last year instead of a ribbon, the judges gave him a coupon for a free therapy session.)

"Principal Turner?"

Principal Turner looked up at me over her clipboard. "Yes, Jeremy?"

"Agatha really needs you to judge hers now, okay? Her uncle's here but he has to leave, so could she go now?"

If the principal was dumb enough to fall for Mr. Jones' whole "uncle" story in the first place, then heck, I was going to milk it for all it was worth.

Principal Turner made a face like she'd just smelled something bad (that would be me). "That's very nice of you, Jeremy, but I really don't think so. It wouldn't be fair to . . ." She checked her clipboard. "Brendan here, who's supposed to go next."

Brendan Weekes was at that moment desperately trying to lure his hermit crab out of its shell for his "Harnessing the Power of Hermit Crabs" demonstration.

"That's okay, Principal Turner," he squeaked, holding out a tempting piece of wilted celery. "I'm good. You go on ahead. I'm fine waiting."

Principal Turner looked at Bitsy Perkins uncertainly. "Well, I suppose . . . if Brendan doesn't mind."

"I don't mind!" Brendan squeaked again. His hermit crab made an angry swipe with his claw and then withdrew back into his shell.

"Fine, let's go see Agatha Hotchkins' project." The judges nodded to each other and started toward Agatha.

I raced on ahead. "Agatha, go!" I yelled.

Agatha, who had been distracted watching Mr. Jones and the Suits descend on her, snapped to attention.

It was all or nothing.

Principal Turner and the other judges gathered around Agatha's table just as Mr. Jones arrived, wire cage in hand.

"Go ahead, Agatha," Principal Turner said.

"Take these two into custody." Mr. Jones signaled to two Mr. Suits flanking him on either side. But before they could move, Principal Turner silenced him with her most steely principal stare. I was impressed. (And frightened. I have to go to school with this lady.)

"If you please," she said frostily. "Agatha, proceed."

The Suits shifted, but at Mr. Jones' signal, they hung back.

Agatha gave a nervous smile. "Okay, this year, I knew I needed to do something extra special for the science fair. So for my project, I've created . . ." She whipped the sheet off of the cage with a flourish. "A jackalope."

17.

Agatha Ruins Her Reputation

There was a collective gasp and stunned silence as everyone leaned forward and peered into the cage. Then the quiet murmuring began. And tittering.

Hortense stood up, bared her orange fangs, and raked her pipe cleaner antlers across the top of the cage. She looked very menacing.

Mrs. Marlowe the science teacher gave Agatha a pained look. She knew the signs of impending mental breakdown when she saw them. "Agatha, honey, that's not a jackalope."

Agatha rolled her eyes. "Okay, you're right. It's just an animal hybrid. We used the DNA from an axis deer for the traditional jackalope antler effect."

"Agatha, honey . . ." Mrs. Marlowe started.

"I've got my notebook with my work right here. It's all here—the whole procedure." Agatha pulled the notebook from the night before out of her backpack. She'd even managed to get most of the bloodstains off of the cover. She opened it and held it up. It was filled with all kinds of numbers and gibberish. It looked convincing to me, but heck, a calculus notebook would've convinced me just as much.

Principal Turner made a mark on her clipboard. "I'm sorry, Agatha, but it's clear that what you have here is just a rabbit with pipe cleaners on his head. It is not a jackalope. Not by any stretch of the imagination." She turned to the other judges.

"Shall we move along?" She shooed Bitsy Perkins on to the next project and gave Mrs. Marlowe, who had taken Agatha's notebook and was reading it carefully, a stern look.

Hortense spat at them in disgust and pooed in her cedar chips.

Principal Turner stopped momentarily in front of my planetary disaster. "Whose is this?"

I raised my hand. "Mine."

"Pluto's no longer a planet, son. Might want to change it before we get back to you." They headed back to Brendan, whose hermit crab was now out of his shell and attempting to swing a tiny hammer hard enough to ring the bell at the top of a pole.

"Yeah, okay," I muttered.

"So, you think you're cute, do you?" Mr. Jones had my arm in a vise grip before I'd even turned back around.

I've used that expression "So-and-so has murder in his eyes" and I thought I knew what it looked like. Turns out, I'd never really seen it until I looked at Mr. Jones right then. We'd really played him for an idiot, and he knew it. And he was going to make us pay.

"We should've just been straight with you," I said apologetically, trying not to look at the handcuffs Mr. Jones had taken out. "But we didn't know how to tell you."

"Twitchett isn't an inventor, he's a con artist. Hortense is all he ever had," Agatha said. "She's my bunny, and he stole her. I had some notes to make a jackalope, and Twitchett stole them. He was working some kind of online scam—I think he was trying to con some international buyers."

I did my eye contact thing. "He never had what it takes to make an actual jackalope," I said. Which if you think about it, was true. "And we sure don't—we're not even in high school yet." I kept my eyes locked on Mr. Jones's face. I didn't want to see Agatha's expression when I said that. "I don't know if Bob and Mrs. Simmons were part of his con or whether he was conning them too, but when I came home the other night, he'd stashed Hortense in my room."

"Besides," Agatha said. "Even if he had done what he said, it wouldn't have been a real jackalope anyway, just an animal hybrid. But if any rabbit has a jack-alope temperament it's Hortense, right, Hortense?" She poked a pencil between the bars of the cage and Hortense attacked it with gusto.

"And you expect me to believe this?" Mr. Jones stared into my eyes so hard that I half expected a photo-copy of my brain to come out of his butt. "You've been running all over the city with this in your suitcase? Just an overgrown rabbit?"

He pointed a finger at Hortense, who looked offended at his tone.

"You didn't even tell us who you were! We were just trying to get a minute to figure things out. We didn't know who to trust." I didn't even try to put on the pathetic face— I was afraid one wrong move would be it for us.

"I'm not a fool." Mr. Jones grabbed me by the shoulder and turned me around, pulling my hands behind my back. I could practically feel the steel on my wrists. "You two AND your jackalope are under—"

"Jones, you've got to see this." Mr. Suit #2 hurried over and pointed to a nearby table where the judges were gathered. I gritted my teeth. Carter Oliver.

"You two don't move," Mr. Jones barked at us and followed Mr. Suit #2 over to the table. Naturally, me and Agatha followed them. It probably would've been a good time for us to make our escape, but heck, I had to see what had just saved my hide (at least temporarily).

Carter's table had a fish tank on it with a huge but otherwise normal-looking goldfish inside the middle of it. The fish was swimming around, doing regular goldfish things, when suddenly, without any warning, it disappeared. (Except for a little trail of nondisappearing goldfish poo. Apparently, even Carter couldn't do everything.)

There was a collective "oooh" from the crowd gathered around the table. I rolled my eyes. Please. Like they've never seen a disappearing fish before.

Principal Turner put down her clipboard and leaned forward, getting so close to the tank that her nose was almost touching the glass. "Where'd he go?"

Carter Oliver smirked and snapped his fingers. The goldfish reappeared. The crowd, apparently working from a script, went with a collective "aaah." Carter held up a remote control. "Want to see it again?"

What a suckup.

The crowd packed in tighter, but I'd seen enough. Besides, I could tell from the crowd's lines what was happening. *Ooh* for disappearing fish, *aah* for reappearing. Terrific.

The Mr. Suit types had stopped watching and were all talking into their cuffs or on their earphone thingies. They were totally ignoring us. Which was fine by me, but still. Come on. Fake jackalope over here.

Agatha came up to me, holding Hortense's head-band. "Want to be a jackalope?" She held it out to me.

"No thanks. I don't feel like going on the run again any time soon."

Agatha grinned. I tried to smile back, but I didn't want to get my hopes up. We weren't in the clear yet. "And Jack?"

"In Hortense's cage at home wearing a turban on his head. We're good."

I nodded and turned back to the Carter Show.

Carter had apparently finished his presentation, because the crowd around the table burst into a huge round of applause. I threw up in my mouth a little. I think Agatha ground a couple of her back teeth into dust.

Guess we didn't need to wonder who would take the big prize this year. I felt pretty bad for Dewey Childress, who was up for judging next. I don't care how hopped-up on sugar water his rats were getting—that project was toast.

Mrs. Marlowe didn't even bother to check out the hopped-up rats, though. She pushed her way out of the crowd and pulled Agatha aside.

"Your project isn't going to win, Agatha," she said apologetically. Well, duh. And yeah, I was eavesdropping. Big deal. "But I have to say, I'm very impressed with your calculations here." She handed Agatha back her notebook.

"You are?" Agatha stopped trying to incinerate Carter's hair with her eyes and perked up a little.

"I know you weren't able to test your theories in the lab, but there is some solid reasoning here. I almost believe it would have worked!" Mrs. Marlowe laughed.

"Thanks!" Agatha looked much more cheery.

"Of course it would be completely unethical and possibly illegal to test it, so we'll never be sure. But come talk to me before school tomorrow. We have some science scholarship programs, you know." She patted Agatha on the shoulder. "And better luck next year."

Mrs. Marlowe turned to leave and gave me a weak smile. "Nice . . . spray painting."

She rejoined the other judges just in time to see Dewey's rat guzzling what looked like Karo syrup.

"You're sure the boy didn't go anywhere but the craft store last night?" The voice was coming from somewhere over my shoulder. I did the bend-down-and-pretend-I'm-tying-my-shoe move and glanced back. It was Mr. Jones and Mr. Suit #2. They looked like they were having some kind of secret meeting. Naturally, I scooched closer.

Mr. Jones was frowning.

Mr. Suit #2 checked his notebook. "Home and back. No outside visitors, no other stops. And we swept the apartment earlier. No suspicious activity."

"And the girl?"

"Didn't leave the building until this morning. No visitors. Apartment swept earlier. And there was nothing in the Simmons place."

Mr. Jones nodded thoughtfully. "Have they apprehended Twitchett yet?" He was watching Carter through narrowed eyes.

Mr. Suit #2 shook his head. "He gave them the slip in Caracas. But there's still time. We'll get him. So Project Jackalope?"

"Project Jackalope is dead. Mark it down as a fraudulent claim," Mr. Jones said. "Now get on the phone with Washington. I want clearance for Project Goldfish and I want it now."

"Got it." Mr. Suit #2 hurried out of the gym as Mr. Jones strolled casually up to Carter.

"So, son, why don't we have a little conversation? Tell me about your project. I have quite a proposal for you."

From my crouch, I watched as Mr. Jones took Carter aside. It didn't take a brain surgeon to know where that was headed. I almost felt sorry for Carter.

Or at least I would've, if he hadn't been such a repulsive egomaniac.

I went back over to Agatha, who was still clutching her notebook and wearing her pipe cleaner antlers, and nudged her in the side.

"Did you hear that?"

"Hear what?"

"Project Jackalope is officially closed."

We high-fived as Principal Turner pinned a blue ribbon on Carter's disappearing fish.

EPILOGUE

I Make a New Friend

So I got a C– on my project, big surprise. It would've been a B–, except I included Pluto, which everybody knows isn't a planet anymore. (Thanks, Dad.)

Carter's not in school anymore, at least not here. He came in the day after the science fair bragging about some big government project he was going to be a part of, and then he never showed up again. The cheerleading squad wore black armbands at the next game. Big loss. I'm crushed.

I didn't hear from Mr. Jones or the rest of the Suits either, which kind of surprised me. Guess they had better things to do, what with Project Goldfish and the whole search for Twitchett. (Last I heard, he was still on the run somewhere in Venezuela.) I'm not complaining, though.

People at school kept clear of me, at least for a little while. Mostly because they were afraid my drug overlord boss might swoop in and shoot it out with me in the bus parking lot. But then I think it dawned on them that a hardened criminal probably wouldn't be such a wuss at volleyball.

It gave me some time to do some heavy-duty thinking, though, mostly about how Jack and Agatha had stuck by me. Heck, Clint Warburton didn't even stick by me when I got caught shooting spitballs in health class. It doesn't take a brainiac to figure out how fast he would've caved with those Suit guys on his tail. Not your definition of an awesome friend. (Well, not mine, anyway.)

And yeah, fine, I've got a soft spot for a jackalope. Big deal, right? So I figured, what the hell? The next day I saved a spot for Agatha at lunch. And I've gone over to her place for some quality Jack time. Heck, I went so wacky that I even visited Killer at Keisha's house. It's not like it's his fault he moved out—he can't help it if he's a big sack of dander who lives in a pink plastic mansion. Me and Keisha even figured out how to wire his hot pink Corvette with a remote, and I swear that rat thinks he's Dale Earnhardt. (Hello, next year's science fair.)

Mrs. Marlowe helped save Agatha's rep, too, which helped nip any lunchtime teasing in the bud. Everybody'd heard about Agatha's lame project, but once Mrs. Marlowe took a class period to explain that Hortense was a stand-in because the real deal would've gotten Agatha arrested, they pretty much got over it. Nick Hurley's even started hanging out and stealing her chips at lunch. (And I know for a fact corn chips make him gag.)

We had a hard time keeping Jack secret at first, even with Hortense protecting him. (Apparently Agatha's mom hates Hortense and keeps clear of her cage at all times.) But once he shed his antlers it got a lot easier. According to Agatha, it's a seasonal thing. (Either that, or we just got a defective jackalope.) We told Agatha's mom that Hortense had spontaneously reproduced, and her mom actually bought it. I know, it makes no sense, but you have to hear Agatha explain it. She made it sound cool and believable, like spontaneous human combustion.

Which brings me to the current problem. I think I should probably take this opportunity to apologize to the entire world for the unleashing of Agatha. If I hadn't come up with that idea about the science fair, Mrs. Marlowe never would've seen Agatha's notebook, and never would've convinced Agatha's mom that Agatha has a future in science. And if she hadn't done that, Agatha wouldn't have been allowed to start up her scientific research again.

Which means I wouldn't be sitting here with the world's only Batterfly sticking its proboscis into my ear. And yes, I said Batterfly—a one-of-a-kind bat/butterfly hybrid, courtesy of Agatha. It was a birthday present. Happy birthday to me.

So I'll just say it one last time, for the record. I'm sorry. Believe me. I'm sorry.

Author's Note

- This is a fictionalized portrayal, but the Defense Advanced Research Projects Agency, or DARPA, is a real agency in the United States Department of Defense.

- It really is working to develop cyborg moths, known as Hybrid Insect Micro-Electro-Mechanical Systems, or HI-MEMS.

- It really is developing one-way-invisible self-healing shoot-through shields as part of the "Asymmetric Materials for the Urban Battlespace" program.

- It really is working on ultrasound mind control helmets for soldiers.

- It really is developing the Energetically Autonomous Tactical Robot, or EATR, a robot that powers itself by consuming organic biomass—although the developers insist that, contrary to early news reports, EATR will feed on organic matter from plants, not humans.

- There really is a flashlight-shaped weapon that induces vomiting. The LED Incapacitator, or "puke ray," produces pulses of multicolored light at a frequency that makes its target barf.

- However, DARPA is not developing an army of killer jack-alopes. Yet.

- For more information about DARPA, you can visit its website at www.darpa.mil (or you can just go to Wikipedia).

Acknowledgments

- Big thanks are in order to everyone who made Project Jackalope a reality.

- To my mom for pointing out the lameness of my original plot and forcing me to rethink it.

- To my Dad, my Mom, my sister Sarah, and my brother-in-law Robert for reading revisions until their eyes crossed.

- To my agent Steve Malk, my editor Julie Romeis, and everyone at Chronicle for working so hard to get *Project Jackalope* into shape.

- To SCBWI and my writing friends for being such a great support system (and so much fun!).

- To everyone at *Wait Wait ... Don't Tell Me!* for helping me discover some of the crazier DARPA stuff.

- And to DARPA for working on such cool things and for having a good sense of humor (fingers crossed).

- To my dog Binky for putting up with delayed walks and dinners and for causing only minor destruction.

- And special thanks to the sea lions at Lincoln Park Zoo for being a bunch of smug show-offs.